Nurse For A Night

by
Barbara Thorn

Dales Large Print Books
Long Preston, North Yorkshire,
England.

British Library Cataloguing in Publication Data.

Thorn, Barbara
  Nurse for a night.

  A catalogue record for this book is
  available from the British Library

  ISBN 1-85389-719-1 pbk

First published in Great Britain by Robert Hale Limited, 1968

Copyright © 1968 by Robert Hale Limited

Published in Large Print 1997 by arrangement with Robert
Hale Limited.

Dales Large Print is an imprint of
Library Magna Books Ltd.
Printed and bound in Great Britain by
T.J. International Ltd., Cornwall, PL28 8RW.

CHAPTER ONE

If there was an explanation for the events occurring that January it doubtless had to do with the unprecedented severity of that winter, for while other things contributed, it was the plummeting temperatures, the wild winds and unusual amount of snowfall and rain that played havoc with so many of the amenities of everyday life which had withstood so many decades of earlier winters.

A prognosticator in Brighton warned that the sea would rise to extraordinary heights all along the British coasts. No one heeded the gentleman for the excellent reason that qualified weathermen scoffed at him. A London statistical organization, going, they said, on available records stretching back several hundred years, had come up with a most unusual notion. Beginning shortly after Christmas Britain would be subjected to one of the most severe buffetings from the weather in her long history.

An interesting idiosyncrasy of human

nature is that people will take some position on every subject under the sun regardless of what they know of the topic, which can usually be said is very little. Someone once said all this was an automatic mental reflex based upon prejudice.

While an axiom as trite as this one is rarely explained by those who bequeath it, everyone else hops in to do precisely that, and in this case at least it must be admitted there was both some truth and great leeway for error, for although most Britons pooh-poohed the idea of a frightful winter simply because they chose not to believe such a thing likely, as a matter of fact the prognosticators were proved correct shortly after the advent of the New Year when a stunning wind of hurricane proportions ripped out roofs, tore away electric lines, upended cars and did an unprecedented amount of damage to a sea-side town.

But Britons are difficult to convince. Some said they had warned against such a happening and the majority simply said nothing at all because one smashed North Sea town hardly constituted a national disaster.

The barometric pressures, though, caused

some former scoffers to become quiet. As January settled in a few uncertain columnists wrote uneasily or with little of the old habitual irony about the prognostications of those whom they had formerly termed fakes and had accused of trying to promote panic.

In Harlham, a village in Suffolk which received an inordinate amount of rainfall on the night of January sixth, Esau Gibbon, a countryman, spread the news that, on the day the storm departed, his rain-gauge had measured three inches of rain in three hours.

Mr John Weldon, proprietor of the Coach and Four, Harlham's pub, said that in forty years he'd never once had a drop of water penetrate his ancient slate roof, but that on the sixth of January three leaks had appeared. No one pointed out that after several centuries Mr Weldon's roof was quite entitled to leak a little.

Will Forman, who owned the chemist's shop and who was a former navy man and therefore, one assumed, accustomed to foul weather, said he'd never seen anything like it; that even those frightful seasonal storms of the South China Sea couldn't compare to the storm that came out of nowhere to hit Harlham on the sixth.

Of course there were others; no one in the village had escaped knowledge of the storm, and equally predictably there were some who muttered darkly about demon influences and the like.

The result, however, was that Harlham had actually received little physical damage, so people were more or less inclined to chalk it up to an unusual storm at a time of year when storms were to be expected, and while they didn't forget about it they nonetheless resumed their normal routines.

As Gordon Johnson, the retired solicitor, said, 'We've all seen storms before; this one may have set up a record rainfall for Harlham but it hardly made history.'

Because, by the eighth of January the sun shone—coldly and inhospitably to be true—people set about cleaning up the rubbish which had been washed into the roads and back-yards of Harlham and adopted Mr Johnson's philosophical viewpoint. It had been a bad 'un all right, but damage had been slight.

The fact that the village of Harlham was very old and therefore constructed largely of stone and timber, both impervious to the elements if properly anchored, gave support to Gordon Johnson's point of view.

The town had undoubtedly received a fierce buffeting but nothing much had been done in the way of physical damage, therefore no real reason for anxiety existed.

The people who vocally or privately considered it likely demonia had something to do with the storm had precedent to rely upon. Harlham being a very ancient village had any number of weird tales. No headless horsemen, nothing of that nature, but earthy legends of witches and the like. Mr Weldon said in his pub one evening that it was scarcely to be expected belted knights could in their Other World trigger such a storm, but even if that were so, why now? Why hadn't they done it two or three hundred years back?

Jenny Malcolm's queerness, a matter of long standing in Harlham, terminated in definite madness on the eleventh of January, which naturally gave a sudden check to all the talk against supernatural forces being at work.

Not among the educated nor the highly literate it is true, but then Harlham, being largely rural and quite insular, didn't possess too many of that class of people. Unless they owned businesses in the town or had retired to the countryside, the people were by and large countrymen who, while by no means un-astute, on the other hand through choice or prejudice were not too widely travelled nor read.

Of course, as was pointed out when they came to take Jenny Malcolm away, the old girl'd been a bit odd for the past twenty-five years; since she'd lost her son and husband in The War. Never violent nor troublesome, just a bit odd.

John Weldon said every village had at least one Jenny Malcolm and he also hinted it was more likely that the middle-years' transition rather than the loss of her men had disturbed her cerebral processes.

No one heeded that. In fact no one actually minded seeing old Jenny taken away. But they did recall something she'd told Mrs Eaton, the ironmonger's wife. Jenny had said Harlham was going to be destroyed as was Sodom—not for the same reason, naturally, for this was Britain—by fire and flood.

At the Coach and Four old Mr Brewster, possessed of a doctorate in philosophy and some years back a noted scholar, disputed the contention that fire and flood had been what had destroyed Sodom. Jeremy Sloat, antithesis of Paul Brewster, said coarsely it made not a damn bit of difference what had destroyed Sodom, the fact was that another bloody storm like the last one striking Harlham would very probably prove loony Jenny correct.

Mr Brewster, whose lovely daughter Patience was the district nurse—paid so it was assumed through some section of the National Health—said indignantly his daughter had treated exactly seven minor injuries arising from the storm, and that was to his way of thinking a far cry from any variety of local disaster. As for future storms he was perfectly confident Harlham would withstand them as it had been withstanding storms for a thousand years—*and* that included another Norman invasion too!

Pat Brewster herself avoided discussion of the storm when possible because by the twelfth of January it had become a sore subject with her father. She called round to look in upon those she'd treated—mostly people struck by flying objects; *earthly* flying objects—and otherwise managed to remain competently busy at her task.

She was a girl of twenty-four with a complexion like country cream. Her hair was brown, worn short; her eyes were also brown, and she had, so the nasty old men of the community decided, the prettiest legs in the county of Suffolk.

As a matter of fact Patience Brewster was an unusually attractive girl. Loose blouses could not hide her most obvious feminine attractions any more than her old sack-like working overcoat and stout walking shoes could detract from the grace and poise of her stride.

She had come to Harlham with her widowed father six years before the present time. It was said she'd left the south country because of a disappointing love affair. *Pat* never said that; in fact she seldom mentioned men in any capacity, but people who had known the Brewsters elsewhere had told the story and it now persisted.

She was an excellent nurse. Mrs Eaton questioned the ambition of a girl who was a professionally trained, state-registered nurse burying herself in a place such as Harlham where the eligible young men either left for London the moment they could, or were the loutish sons of farmers.

But then Mrs Eaton's shrewd observations and sharp tongue had lacerated everyone in the village at one time or another, so no one really paid much attention to what she said about Pat Brewster.

Of course there was Will Forman, the chemist, but it was said he was a misogynist. No one knew where that idea had started but perhaps Mrs Eaton wasn't entirely innocent; at least it had been rumoured that she'd accused Will Forman of hating womenkind and certainly since Will was single although relatively young, some credence was lent to the plausibility.

According to John Weldon—and he surely should have known—Will Forman wasn't actually a woman hater; he simply scorned them as intelligent human beings, an attitude Mr Weldon, a lifelong bachelor of fifty-five, was inclined to find favour with.

But Pat Brewster and John Weldon were friends. She was also a friend to Will Forman, but in a more professional capacity; in the performance of her duties Pat frequently had occasion to patronize Will Forman's shop. In fact it had been predicted several years back that ruggedly handsome Will Forman and Pat Brewster would fall in love.

When this didn't happen, or at least after several years had passed and no indication of it happening had become noticeable, the stories of misogynism had begun. No one had ever thought it might be the other way around; that it wasn't Will who didn't like the opposite sex, it was Pat.

Gallantry was not dead in the rural countryside. Moreover, who could imagine for a moment a girl with as lovely a face, as perfect a figure, as Pat Brewster could dislike men. Obviously no one thought so. Even Gordon Johnson, whose worldliness included a stretch in North America as well as South Africa not to mention his long tenure in sophisticated London, never once appeared to suspect Pat Brewster of being a man-hater. It was too ridiculous; beautiful girls just naturally gravitated towards handsome men.

But the visible fact was to the contrary. Pat rarely went out with men, seldom was seen talking to the younger ones, and while she'd treated those who needed her services in a professional capacity, otherwise she was always friendly, always helpful, and always cold as ice.

14

CHAPTER TWO

By the twelfth of January storm warnings were issued again for coastal towns. This did not directly effect Harlham which was a fair distance inland, but on the other hand, since no British town is more than seventy miles from the sea, coastal storm warnings implied some degree of peril or at least inconvenience inland as well.

As Will Forman commented at the Coach and Four that same evening the difference was a relative one; people could and doubtless would, evacuate some coastal towns while the people of Harlham who'd never abandoned their village even when the Normans had come or when Jerry had flown over dropping bombs, would batten their hatches and ride it out.

John Weldon's pub was the unofficial Town Hall. Harlham had an official set of rooms, of course; nearly every large village had a set, time-hallowed and time-honoured. But in Harlham as much as elsewhere most popular consensus was

15

achieved in the pub. It was the one place where everyone met on equal ground. For example, while Paul Brewster, Ph.D., appeared upon ceremonial days robed and medalled, Jeremy Sloat stood on the sidelines looking exactly what he was, a shaggy-headed, squat, burly countryman without education. In the Coach and Four, however, Jeremy could and frequently did, challenge the erudite wisdom of Mr Brewster and no one excepting Brewster saw anything amiss in it.

They were all there, 'Weldon's Regulars' as the Puritans in the Harlham countryside derisively called them, the night of the twelfth—Frank Eaton, the diffident little rustic ironmonger who there escaped from the waspish tongue of his buxom little wife, among the others. Frank said he hardly expected another 'bad 'un' like the storm that struck on the sixth. His reason was weak but ordinary enough; it had something in common with the adage about lightning never striking twice in the same place. The trouble with it was that lightning had been known on many occasions to strike twice. Still, it was a comfortable and therefore prevalent opinion that night.

John Weldon said that if the worst occurred what was there to fear beyond fear itself; after all their village had withstood the earlier storm. It would most certainly withstand another.

The logician and retired solicitor Gordon Johnson was outraged at this slipshod reasoning. 'Every precaution should be taken,' he growled, and didn't elucidate for the best of all reasons; he'd had four pints of John Weldon's best dark stout and was annoyed by a little difficulty in arranging his thoughts.

'Every precaution,' said Paul Brewster, Member of the Council, 'has been taken.' Brewster peered into his beer mug a moment, then, pricked by conscience, added, 'Of course there isn't much to be done. Keep the drains unclogged; warn people not to be caught out; fasten the doors and shutters.' He raised a cadaverously thin, fine-featured old face as though expecting to be challenged. No one took it up.

'The wireless,' put in Jeremy Sloat from a shadowy corner, 'says there's fresh turbulence about that might blow it all away—out to sea or over to France.'

That evoked a predictable retort. Esau

Gibbon, a rawboned lanky countryman who raised pigs and a few dairy cattle, said he thought it was a capital idea, the blasted storm going over to France. Like most of the other older men Esau Gibbon had been in France two decades earlier and had liked neither the countryside, the people, nor particularly the conditions under which he'd been a transient there.

'Better still,' he said with candid vindictiveness, 'let 'er blow all the way across t'Germany.'

Someone asked Gordon Johnson what liability was involved. Very often, when Gordon was stone sober, his opinion was sought. Not entirely because he'd been such an eminently successful solicitor but because the proof of his superiority lay in the fact that he was also quite wealthy. In the dog-eat-dog legal jungle of London and foreign parts only the very astute survived. Gordon hadn't just survived, he'd retired to the country with a fortune. *That* meant something.

'What liability?' he asked, raising his florid face with the hard little blue eyes. 'It's an act of God. Of course if the pub roof fell in and injured some of us, Mr Weldon would be liable on the grounds that he should've inspected the roof.' The little blue eyes turned sardonic. 'But—Mr Weldon doubtless has liability insurance so we'd be suing a hydra-headed insurance concern and even winning wouldn't ensure victory. The thing would be drawn out for years until we'd all be so heartily sick of it we'd cheerfully settle for a few pounds each. Liability? Humph!'

Jeremy Sloat maliciously said, with the wind rising against the leaded window at his back. 'We couldn't sue God because he's dead. I read 'is obituary in the newspaper.'

No one smiled. It was a poor night for such a quip. Esau Gibbon belched sonorously and John Weldon refilled old Brewster's mug; he also went along to stir the grate and coax a bit more heat from the stove. It was turning a bit cold inside. Outside there was the sound of wind.

Jeremy turned at the sound of tiny fists and watched the first minute droplets of wind-driven rain strike glass. He drew his old tweed jacket close and settled back in his corner again. He had the look in his eye of a man who knew he should be some place other than where he was but who resisted the sense of duty because he was comfortable. When Weldon cocked an eyebrow Jeremy nodded for the refill.

'Blasted country anyway,' he snarled as John poured. 'In South Africa they had sunshine three hundred days a year.'

'Yes,' conceded old Brewster acidly, 'and it's no proper place for an Englishman.'

'Isn't it?' challenged Jeremy settling back with his mug. 'There's thousands out there living well.'

'Not for long they won't,' snapped Brewster. 'It's an inhuman system they've got. Mark my words: it'll come crashing down round their heads one of these days'

Jeremy mumbled something sounding like, 'Damned old anarchist,' and noisily drank.

The wind picked up a little. Without commenting or even perhaps consciously being aware, every man in the room listened. There was no moaning, no rattling of roof-slates, no banging of loosened slats or doors or shutters but in their private and secret minds they knew these things would be along.

Esau changed position; went over and settled into the gloomy corner near Jeremy Sloat. He perhaps felt better being with another farmer. He said something about the animals out in the fields this night. Jeremy glumly nodded without comment. He seemed to still be thinking of the blandishments of a place where the sun shone three hundred days a year.

Paul Brewster called for one more round and took out his pocket-watch to consult with it. The hour was not late but there were some telly programmes he was addicted to. Very shortly now they'd be appearing. Pat would have a nice fire going too. He tucked away the watch, fell to thinking of his beautiful daughter, and after a while said, 'It's a matter of the variety of storms a man feels himself best suited to face. Political, spiritual or natural. I prefer natural storms. When they are over the air is washed clean and except for picking up the debris it is all over.'

Jeremy raised little shrewd eyes. He seemed to be of the opinion this statement had somehow been directed against him; against his manhood in fact. He might have started another argument with old Brewster except that burly Will Forman, perhaps the youngest and most certainly the most widely travelled and physically powerful man in the room, spoke up first.

21

'It's not all over,' he contradicted bluntly. 'That last one took out my big front window. Insurance covered it but not the damage done by water inside the shop.' Will sat hunched at the little bar. 'I've seen South Africa and a lot of other places; here is where I was born and here is where I hope to die. Nothing patriotic about it. It's the best place on earth to me, storms and bad weather included.' He looked down where old Brewster sat listening. 'Anyway there's no natural storm that doesn't stir up the other two kinds also.' Forman twisted to let loose a barb at Jeremy too. 'South Africa is desert. You've got to have rain otherwise you get all that sunshine and you can't grow a decent crop of anything.'

No one pursued this, probably because the others, excepting Sloat and Brewster, felt it made sense, but more probably because South Africa wasn't among their immediate and local concerns. That wind was flinging particles of earth against the windows now, which meant it was building up to the same strength of the former wind on the sixth when the first frightful storm hit Harlham.

John Weldon glanced askance at his wall-clock. It wasn't closing time; in fact

22

it wasn't even close to it, but all the same he was wearying of the gloom inside his Coach and Four. He was well up in years, a leathery, stringy individual to whom it seemed life didn't actually vary but rather endlessly repeated itself bringing a man eventually to an imperturbable acceptance that everything he'd done or seen would come round again before he died. This attitude had made John well nigh unflappable.

'Let 'er come,' he said into the silence of the warm little poorly lighted room. 'We had 'er on the sixth and no matter what the oldtimers says I'll bet Harlham's seen dozens as bad since it was founded. No record of the place being razed.'

Paul Brewster's head shot up. He cast a glance to where Weldon stood as though appalled at this pragmatism. 'And if the place is razed tonight what will you say tomorrow, John? That it no doubt happened before and no one bothered to record it? What difference could that possibly make to us who will bear the brunt of it?'

Weldon gazed quietly to where old Brewster was hunched at the bar. 'All right, old cock,' he said, 'and what good's sitting about like a bunch of dying crows dripping gloom going to do?'

Brewster had no answer. There *was* no answer. Weldon poured himself a glass of ale and banged it on top of his bar as though defying any of them to dispute his attitude. None did.

Frank Eaton was the first to rise, button his coat, settle the cap on his head firmly and step forth to drop some small coins next to John Weldon's glass. He said 'good night' and went out. The moment he opened the door a great gust of stinging wet wind sprang inside. Eaton had no time to look apologetic he had to concentrate on dragging the heavy oak door closed after himself.

Until that moment, while they were all very cognisant of the surly weather out in the night, they'd had no first-hand meeting with it. Now they had and without exception their eyes slewed round to John Weldon's old copper and brass barometer, memento of some long-gone sailing vessel. The spidery black finger was hanging steadily near the chin of a puff-cheeked Neptune who was blowing up a terrible storm, having already passed completely down across the straining face.

Will Forman said, 'Bad night at sea,' and smiled a little at old Neptune behind the glass as though they, and only they, understood what horrors lurked behind those simply stated, undramatic four words.

Esau Gibbon rose and began slowly to button his coat. He looked at Sloat a time or two as though waiting for Jeremy to agree to go out with him. Sloat made no such move, so eventually lanky Esau yanked the cap down over his ears, fished out a woollen scarf which he dexterously wound about his scrawny neck and made for the door.

The same thing happened again, only this time Will climbed off his stool to go to stand by a window peering out.

There was no moon, the sky seemed to have dropped straight down without a break in it anywhere—which was what Will had been searching for—and between heaven and earth there was just room enough for that increasing wind to race along with unrelenting velocity. It could have been so powerful because of that compression, or it could simply be blowing itself out over the land after having whipped the sea into mile-high waves and dirty froth.

Will returned in silence to the bar, finished his drink, plunked down a coin and turned to depart. By this time none of them any longer had much to say. Whatever personal or private concerns ordinarily motivated them, the increasing unearthly scream of the wind had blotted out. None of them doubted for a moment that the sixth of January was about to be re-enacted upon Harlham one week later.

CHAPTER THREE

For Pat Brewster, whose depth of tolerance and strength was unsuspected by the townspeople, the storm of the sixth had been an unnerving experience. If she hadn't shown terror it hadn't been because she hadn't known it. The entire affair and its immediate aftermath had been an angonizing ordeal for her. As she sat at home, now, waiting for her father to return from the Coach and Four listening to the television newsmen, that same slow dread was building up in her again.

The house was of stone and timber,

very old and sheltered on both sides by other stone houses of an equal antiquity. Although the wind blew steadily after six o'clock and the sky darkened swiftly, deep inside the house there was no sensation of storminess at all. Patience Brewster remained in the parlour, which was the central room, being on the ground floor with other rooms flanking it.

Upstairs in one of the two small bedrooms the sounds were fierce and growing fiercer but she only went up there to put on her cardigan before building the fire. She loved seeing and smelling a glowing fireplace. Her father had taught her that addiction—and it was an addiction instead of a convenience; a fireplace on a cold or stormy evening was the best therapy on earth for the primaeval fears lurking in the secret places of every man's heart and mind.

She sat beside the fire straining to hear that which she didn't want to hear until the fire worked its magic and turned her drowsy.

She knew as surely as she was sitting there, someone would have need of her services this night. She was resigned to going out. In fact it wasn't being out in the storm that made her uneasy. It was waiting for something—she knew not what—to happen, that scratched down each nerve. She watched a solemn young man repeating the storm warning with her restlessness mounting. She told herself the uneasiness was fear of a roof falling in, a wall toppling, a series of implosions bursting windows.

She also told herself she could well imagine how such a night must have worked on the completely unenlightened superstitions of her ancestors, compelling them to people the night with demons.

The room warmed quickly. Stone walls and a low ceiling helped immeasurably. She got a book, turned down the volume of the television set, tucked both feet under her in a large easy chair next to the fireplace and settled herself to read. Her father would be along shortly now.

The ironmonger's wife telephoned saying her husband had fallen over a piece of furniture entering the house and she'd like to have Pat look at his shins.

It was one of those nagging calls; the kind people had only come to make when medical services had become nationalized. She told Mrs Eaton unless her husband was

28

seriously injured, which seemed improbable if all she'd told Pat had been the sum total of his accident, she thought Mrs Eaton could do as good a job for her Frank as Pat could do.

It wasn't a very polite rejoinder but she could be quite impolite with people of Mrs Eaton's calibre when the need arose. Furthermore, she was protected by the nursing association which'd had to define a positive policy for both malingerers and the wives of malingerers. So if an irate Mrs Eaton wrote in about Pat's impertinence, it would avail the Eatons nothing.

Her father arrived looking as though he'd exhausted his reserves just in reaching the house, which he admitted was precisely what it'd taken to get home. 'That wind must be sixty to seventy miles an hour,' he told her. 'Do take a look out, Pat; the sky is as black as midnight down upon the village.'

She took his coat and hat to hang them in a cupboard. She returned to ask about tea. He declined on the grounds that he was already half a-wash with John Weldon's stout.

'And that insufferable lout Sloat was there again. I tell you, Patience, the confounded man deliberately baits me. It's the age-old antagonism louts feel for their betters. It used to be the surliness of a clod for a gentleman. Now it's the jealousy of the countryman for the educated person.'

She told him of Mrs Eaton's call. He thought she'd done precisely right, settled into his favourite chair to watch the television set, and told her the ironmonger had probably tumbled over his settee or whatever it had been because he'd been tanked up with John Weldon's beer.

She felt much better now that her father was at home. Just why that should be wasn't explainable; he'd have been utterly useless in any physical emergency. He was tall and as thin as a rail, not to mention physically incapable at his advanced age of contributing much at any time. Of course she'd been concerned when he'd been out in the storm, but he no longer was; he was perfectly safe now so perhaps part of her pleasure was simply relief.

The television set went dead half an hour after he'd arrived home. That upset him. One of the farm women telephoned somewhat later to whine out a rambling almost incoherent complaint of a deep back ache. Finally, as they were having a quiet conversation before the fire, Will Forman called to say he'd like to come round if she didn't mind. Of course she didn't mind, only she was mystified; Will had never done this before and while the call unquestionably had to do with either his calling or hers, it was certainly a frightful night for visiting unless one absolutely had to.

She returned to the parlour, told her father Will was coming over and he, holding an unopened book in his lap, raised pale, quizzical eyes. But he made none of the expected nor obvious inquiries saying instead. 'He picked a fine night, wouldn't you say?'

She smiled, 'Probably someone's hurt or ill. He's coming to take me off somewhere.'

'If you have to go I'd say he'd be the one to have as escort. Strong as a bull, and at times I'm convinced just as hard-headed.'

They smiled at one another. She slipped into her shoes, took away a cup and saucer left over from when she'd earlier had tea alone, then returned to sit by the fire with her book again.

Her father, watching all this, let her get

seated then said, 'It's been several years now, Pat...'

She seemed to know instantly what that meant for she raised her gold-flecked dark eyes, sat a moment without answering as though communications through telepathy, and ultimately said, 'I told you...as far as I'm concerned that ended it.'

'That's not reasonable, Patience,' he protested. 'Those things happen; you're mature, intelligent and educated enough to realize that. He was a fraud. Actually, you were fortunate to discover it when you did. Imagine how terrible it might have been otherwise.'

She listened with the look of a girl who'd heard it all before; a patient, dutiful daughter. When he went on, touching upon a fresh subject, she'd also heard that before.

'The point is, daughter, one rotten apple hardly indicates the entire barrelful is spoilt.'

She gave the same answer she'd given before. 'I realize all that, father, and it's not that I've become a woman who despises all men. I'm simply not interested in any at the moment.'

Paul Brewster threw up his hands.

'Patience, we both know that's not it. And I warn you, child, keep on the way you're going and you'll end up—'

'A spinster,' she said, quoting him. 'What Homer or someone called a "stale virgin". All right; *now* may we just read?'

She dropped her head to the book she held. Her father made no move to do the same but instead kept studying her lowered head, the rounded shoulders, the skirt drawn taut around her thighs as she sat in the chair, the sweet mouth turning astringent. There were perhaps a hundred thousand young men within one day's drive of Harlham who'd have put their hearts at her feet. And simply because she had a livid scar across her heart from one whelp, she was cold towards all men.

A father, particularly one who'd had his child rather late in life, felt an urgency other people did not feel; he desired above all else to see his daughter married to a good man before he died. It was almost an obsession and he recognized it as such, feeling it to be perfectly natural—which of course it was.

She was a wonderful girl. True, she rarely laughed now as she once had, and true again, she had loved with all the ripe and surging passion of which her kind was unstintingly capable, but to look at her since that time one would think she'd already lived her full life.

Paul Brewster's opinion of Harlham was not high. His opinion of the people roundabout left something to be desired. It wasn't that he was arrogant, it was simply that as a good pragmatist, he was utterly realistic—a man who called a spade a spade. A truly honest person.

But as he'd told Pat more than once, he hadn't retired to the country expecting to finish off his last days in the company of intellectuals, for obviously there's never been intellectuals who were native countrymen who remained countryfied. The only permanent country-men were those privately, secretly, fearful of competition, conscious of definite inferior-ity, sure to be gobbled up by citymen—and they knew it.

On the other hand, however, old Brewster had thought there might be a *few* worthwhile intellects, and all he'd come up with had been Will Forman, so much his junior they scarcely even spoke the same language, or Gordon Johnson, who drank more than was good for him, was irascible, and discouraged close friendships.

Someone—or some*thing*—struck the front door a stout blow giving old Brewster a start and causing Pat to lose her place in the book she was reading. The same strike was repeated.

'Let him in before he breaks down the door,' old Brewster said waspishly. 'No need to use a club to announce oneself, drat it.'

She crossed over, went out into the tiny entry and opened the door. It was like casually opening a floodgate. Wind and rain flung the door and her with it half around. If it hadn't been for the powerful arm of Will Forman she'd have received a hard blow from the door. When they closed it he had to lean to help. Straightening round afterwards to remove his crushed hat and coat, both glistening with rain, he said, gazing at her rosy cheeks, 'That wasn't the brightest thing you ever did. Didn't you know that storm's tearing the guts out of things?'

The term 'guts' as well as his forthrightness, warranted or not, made her recoil, then flare out at him. 'I've managed that door before, Mr Forman. I'd have managed it this time. There's no need to be upset.'

He finished shedding hat and coat. 'Isn't there?' he said, and paused to gaze into the parlour where her father sat, where the fire cheerily burned, where warmth and peace prevailed. With his voice under control he said, 'Not in here there isn't, but everyone's not so fortunate. That storm is raising Cain tonight, Pat.'

She wasn't mollified at all but she did appreciate his effort at control. 'Please come into the parlour. Can I get you some tea?'

'Scotch and water please,' he said, turning his back on her and walking in where Paul Brewster sat looking quizzically up into his strained, tight face with the sheen of rain still upon it.

'How is it?' the older man inquired.

'Purgatory,' said Will Forman. 'Only Dante never captured the essence of a real tornado.'

Brewster stirred uneasily. 'I see. There's no occasion for Pat to go out in it, I hope.'

Forman took a chair when invited to do so, saying, 'You can bet your money she'll

36

be called to do so before morning.'

Brewster showed distress. 'I hope not. After all, she's not capable of—'

'That's why I'm here,' said Will, settling back, relaxing a little at a time. 'I thought she'd have to go so I came along to keep vigil with her, and when the call comes to go with her.'

Old Brewster searched Forman's handsomely rugged, rough hewn features. 'I see,' he said quietly, and looked round when his daughter appeared with a scotch and water in one hand, a cup of tea for her father in the other hand. He watched Will take the drink, watched his tough lips part as he thanked her with no real warmth, and he sighed. Will Forman was hardly what would in sophisticated circles be termed a gentleman, but he was knowledgeable, practical, honest and hard-working. A very eligible man with all youth's soft illusions knocked out of him. Old Brewster had got to the point where he'd have accepted Will Forman as a son-in-law with an enormous sigh of relief. At least that's how he felt at the moment, when both Pat and Will seemed passive and Paul Brewster was the only aggressive one.

CHAPTER FOUR

Will Forman was not noted as a conver-
sationalist. He was as good a pharmacist
as there was; much better than was needed
in a village the size of Harlham where
he'd come back to settle down. Paul
Brewster had heard it from Patience,
who'd had it from several highly qualified
medical practitioners, that Will could have
commanded his own salary in London or
in Manchester. But of course old Brewster
knew Will well enough to realize he'd never
move permanently to either place.

The scotch and water loosened him
somewhat, but Brewster still had to prompt
things to keep the visit from deteriorating
into a prolonged, awkward silence for them
all. But after something like half a century
of handling people of all types and ages,
Paul Brewster was fully capable; he might
get sleepy after a while, but otherwise he
could keep the visit on a social level easily
enough. For example, he asked if Will had
ever seen a storm to equal the one outside.

38

Will had, several times in fact. He described a typhoon he'd once been compelled to ride out on a ship in the vicinity of the Chinese mainland. And another wild storm experienced on a run across the wintertime North Atlantic towards Newfoundland.

Pat went to fetch another log. The fire spluttered a brief shower of sparks then settled down to eating its bright way into the fresh wood. Will watched her movements and old Brewster watched him watching Pat. He showed a brooding resentment, or something close to it. Brewster winced inwardly; evidently Will and his daughter'd had an argument. If he knew Pat—and he did—then it was safe to assume she'd chilled Will Forman precisely as she'd done other young and eligible men.

He pushed that thought out of his head and suggested another scotch and water. Will smiled at him. 'You saw me at Weldon's tonight. One scotch is quite enough.' The rock-hard blue eyes twinkled. 'One more—I won't be able to hit the ground with my hat.'

Brewster smiled, not at the joke but at the loose, relaxed amiability Forman was showing. He had indeed seen Will knock back his share of beer this night. He privately thought a spot of drink made Will less withdrawn and he liked him better this way.

There was one thing about Forman some villagers did not especially cotton to; he'd sit, looking a cold challenge, and tell them exactly what he thought of them, of Harlham, of their superstitions, their stuffiness, then he'd heap oil on those troubled waters by saying stuffiness and pigheadedness were national characteristics. Once, when a riled Jeremy Sloat had asked why, if he thought so little of Britain and the British, he'd bothered to come back, Forman had said, 'To make a nick in the national flesh, my friend. To stick a sliver into your damned thick hides and help you come out of it.'

Brewster had been in the Coach and Four that evening—it had been a rare hot night the summer previous—and had expected Sloat, notoriously short-tempered, to take umbrage. But Sloat hadn't, although from that time on he'd never cared much for Will. Nor had a few others in the village.

Brewster himself was wary around the

pharmacist. Not that he anticipated ever being tested in an argument—as a university professor he'd held his own with some of the best minds—but he'd always rather liked something in Forman he couldn't quite describe, and therefore chose to have him as a friend rather than as an adversary. He was honest enough, also, to know himself: He did not like being challenged, never forgot—nor forgave—a challenger. He didn't want to have that feeling towards Forman.

Pat mentioned something to the effect that the telly wasn't functioning. Will eyed the grey-bulging optic and said he shouldn't be surprised; that it would be more astonishing if any of the sets in Harlham were operative since the wind had littered the road with antennae. He then said if she wished he'd go out and jury-rig the thing, although it'd only blow away again.

She looked surprised that he should make the offer. It would be dangerous trying to set the aerial up again on top of the roof. 'We have a radio,' she murmured, and kept eyeing Forman.

'It won't make you feel any better,' he told them. 'I was listening to mine before

41

I came over here. All they're saying is that the storm centre is passing inland directly towards us.'

Pat's father considered the fire for a moment before asking a question. 'You say there are telly aerials in the roads. Is there anything else? I mean, has there been any serious damage, Will?'

Forman's lips parted in a wolfish smile. 'For one thing that glass window in my shop burst inward again. Of course the insurance company will replace it—then cancel my policy. Otherwise, except for bits of roof-slate flying like shrapnel I didn't notice much. Weldon's elegant sign has been torn away and Frank Eaton's wire gates have been ripped from the posts. I suppose out in the country there'll be roofs off barns and whatnot, but I can't say for sure about any of that. I'll tell you this much, though. Anyone trying to drive a car tonight will end up in a ditch or get turned completely over.'

'Frightful,' murmured Paul Brewster looking at his daughter. The old clock on the mantel-piece struck eleven, the fire surged outwards for the first time, driven to do that by a down-plunging gust of wind in the chimney, and the telephone rang, startling them all.

Forman straightened in his chair. Old Brewster's face tightened. Pat went out to answer it in the entrance hall and for the first time they all heard the screech of wind across the rooftop. Something rather like a sharp gunshot sounded too, somewhere out in the night, and that heightened the tension. Apparently a door or gate had been broken loose out there.

When Pat came back she said the call had been from someone at the telephone exchange wishing to determine whether or not their particular line was still working.

'She said some of the other lines were not.'

Pat didn't return to her chair but asked if they'd like anything to eat. Forman, watching her, said, 'Not I, thank you, and if you eat I'd suggest not very much.'

She looked straight at him. 'So as not to be sleepy, is that it?'

'Right,' he agreed, then, at the look in her eyes he said. 'Don't blame me, Pat. *I* had nothing to do with bringing in this storm.'

She instantly relented. 'I'm sorry, Will. Did it show that much?'

He smiled slightly. 'It showed.'

Her father said he'd like some of the oatmeal biscuits she'd baked, and as she went to get them he told Will what an unusually good cook she was. Will looked tart about that.

'What good'll it do, Mr Brewster?'

And although her father knew exactly what Will had meant he affected not to and said, 'Whatever do you mean?'

'You know what I mean. Who'll she ever cook for?'

Brewster's blood-pressure rose a notch. 'If you mean—a husband—don't lament anything until it's a fact.'

'Nice rhetoric,' growled Will, looking the older man directly in the eye. 'Only in her case it's wasted. Tell me something, Mr Brewster—it's none of my business and you'll probably tell me so—but what in the devil has made her so cold and unresponsive?' Evidently Will saw the flash of temper because he raised a hand quickly, as though to defend himself, and said, 'Steady now, Mr Brewster; I'm not asking out of any curiosity. I'm asking out of honest interest.' Will glanced swiftly towards the door through which Pat had disappeared, swung back and said in an intense, swift voice, 'I only half told the

44

truth when I said I was staying in Harlham because I was born here. Your daughter is the other reason....'

Old Brewster's sharp retort died in his throat. The anger stirring in his breast turned to ash. He fingered the book in his lap. She'd be returning any moment. He finally said, 'No doubt there's gossip about her having once been in love.'

'There is.'

'It's true. She had her heart broken years ago, shortly before we moved to Harlham. In fact that was one of the reasons why I came here; fresh surroundings you see.'

'But my God that's been...!'

'I know how long it's been, man,' snapped old Brewster, darting another look towards the pantry doorway. 'Don't you think I'd like to see her get over it? Damnation, I'm old, Mr Forman. I don't want to die with her left—'

He bit it off when Pat came through the doorway with a plate of biscuits. If she noticed how the two men sank back at her approach, breaking off whatever they'd been saying, she gave no indication of it as she offered the plate to her father, first, then to their guest. Only when her eyes met the eyes of Will showing a dark mocking expression, was it clear that she'd guessed.

A moment later the telephone rang again. This time all three of them jumped. Forman smiled and Pat smiled back as she went to answer. During that interim the men sat looking at one another. This time, their eyes seemed to say, she would be called out.

Will ate a biscuit, had a second one and turned impatiently when she didn't reappear. Her father took this opportunity to finish what he'd been saying before. He leaned forward to do this.

'I hope you never have a daughter, Mr Forman.'

Will's slaty gaze was ironic. 'I may never have *anything* Mr Brewster. I'm past thirty. That's not very old granted, but most men are married by then.'

'Yes. I am aware of that.'

'I've never been in any hurry. I'm not in a hurry now. But at least I've found someone I'd *like* to marry, Mr Brewster, and I've never done that before.'

'Pat?'

'Pat!'

Old Brewster settled back in his chair not as pleased as he perhaps should have

46

been, but then not many fathers ever believed some young man is really worthy of their daughter when they come face to face with it. Still, Brewster had a more compelling reason for wanting to see his daughter married than most fathers so he sat and dolefully thought, ultimately agreeing that Will would, in fact, be a good husband, a fair parent, a decent provider. He chided himself, too, for only an hour or two earlier he'd thought of Will in that capacity and had been wishful.

Pat returned, stood nearby gazing at their glum faces and said, 'It's Joan Eaton. That was her husband. She's been taken very ill. He couldn't describe the symptoms very well. In fact he sounded almost incoherent but then the telephone line wasn't very good. In any case it sounded rather like an abdominal attack of some kind.' She was looking directly at her father when she concluded with: 'Of course I'll have to go.'

Will arose, brushed biscuit crumbs off and said, 'I knew it would happen. I simply expected it sooner. Pat—supposing it's appendicitis?'

She was cool. 'Suppose it's only indigestion? Will, you don't have to come and

I do appreciate your offer.'

He grinned, striding out into the hall for his damp hat and coat. 'Get into your waterproof,' he growled back at her, 'and let's be going.'

CHAPTER FIVE

They all knew the storm was bad. With the exception of Will none of them had been out in it recently but they had the memory of the previous storm to give them an idea of what lay beyond the door.

Old Brewster went into the hall with them, watched his daughter get into her rain coat and wellingtons, then asked if this wasn't expecting too much of her.

She was gentle towards him in replying, saying that he knew perfectly well she'd have to go; that he had brought her up knowing full well each person had his duty and his obligation. Then she kissed him and turned towards Will, who had one hand on the door-knob, the other hand pushed into a pocket.

She smiled tentatively. 'Ready, Will.'

Then she said, 'You'd think we were being launched to the moon.'

He didn't reply but opened the door, caught her by the arm and propelled her through the narrow opening. He then also stepped through, never once releasing the door, and tugged mightily to get it closed from the outside.

Pat was flung against a dripping stone wall on her left, the breath ruthlessly sucked out of her. She raised a hand instinctively, and discovered this was how best to breathe for otherwise the storm created such suctions it was nearly impossible to keep any breath in one's lungs.

Getting off the stone front of the house required another effort. She and Will could not communicate except through touch and, occasionally, an exchanged look.

The wind screamed round corners, plummeted down over rooftops, raced up roadways with the speed—and sound—of locomotives. It carried rain with it, each drop shredded into pin-head needles of wild spray.

There was no way to determine where the sky was. Even when Will dragged her stumbling into a recessed doorway to catch her breath, and she looked up, the

49

blackness seemed only an arm's distance away. It could have been heaven or it could have been just the terrible darkness.

They hadn't come very far but her legs trembled, her lungs pumped for air they could retain, her eyes watered and deep inside she felt the labouring of her heart.

Will stood in front as though protecting her from the storm. All around them the village lay cowed and glistening. The roadway had some litter, mostly television aerials although there were also some torn shutters and a few shredded signs including the one belonging above the door of John Weldon's Coach and Four inn.

It seemed to her they couldn't possibly reach the Eaton residence which lay to the north where Frank Eaton's iron-yard lay. She tapped Will's shoulder. When he turned she pulled him close enough to whisper and said, 'We can't go down the main road, Will. There's no protection—it'll blow us off our feet.'

He gripped her upper arms, put his lips to her ear and said, 'As soon as you're rested we'll cut around and get into the alley behind Weldon's. It's narrow, the buildings are higher, and we should have enough protection.'

It made sense. She leaned a little to look. His face was inches from hers. Just for a moment she watched his eyes widen, his face loosen, then he shoved her away almost roughly and set his back to her again for as long as it took to determine their onward course. Then, when she pushed a hand into his to hold on, signifying she was prepared, he lunged out into the storm again.

The most unnerving factor was the screeching, the endless rising and falling howl of wind. There were other sounds less noticeable such as the clap of broken shutters and the pistol-like sharp sound when a brittle bit of slate from a rooftop struck pavement nearby. As Will had told them back at the house, it was like shrapnel. If one of those pieces of stone were to hit a person in the temple, the eye, the nose or mouth, the effect would be similar.

She had trouble in breathing, which weakened her. When she began to drag a little after covering only another few yards he turned, pushed her roughly against the front of a building, brought out a scratchy woollen muffler and tied it over her face covering both nose and mouth. At once she found it much easier to breathe. She tried to smile her thanks but he turned, holding her hand, and resumed his fierce fight to make way for them.

At the first corner he had to wait for a particularly bad bit of wind and rain to pass. She squeezed his cold fingers to indicate something—encouragement for one thing, appreciation for another. He turned and gazed at her eyes, squeezed back and turned to push on round the corner.

They didn't have far to go but they had to cross the street where a littered little narrow alley opened darkly, awash with trapped rainwater. As long as they moved a foot at a time keeping very close to the fronts of buildings they were spared the full, roaring force of the squall, but the moment he attempted to step away, to cross the street, it seemed that the wind turned its full fierce power against them. Will staggered, tilted on his heels, fought to get into a crouch and tried again.

Pat's breath caught in her throat. It was like being struck in the side with a blow that never ended. She crept up to get on the upper side of Will, using him as her windbreak. That helped a little but they had to fight with all their strength just to step off the kerb.

The rain could only make their clothing cold and heavy; because their faces were lowered it didn't sting them as hard now as it had before. But the galeforce wind tore at them unmercifully.

She stumbled when they were several feet from the kerb. He wouldn't have known except that, gripping her hand, he felt the tug, halted and turned, then gave a strong pull that got her up again.

She thought she would strangle, that her weight was going to prove inadequate, that she'd be swept away. She probably would have at least fallen, perhaps been rolled helplessly along, except for his sheltering body and physical strength. He fought her rising panic and the storm simultaneously.

She was deafened by the dinning scream, by the shrieks as wind struck sharp corners and was torn by them, by the great moaning as slipstreams broke upon rooftops and went soaring away. It did not occur to her that the major power of the storm was ten feet above her; that if it had been any lower she'd have been tumbled in it like a leaf.

Will never stopped fighting. Once, through eyes pinched nearly closed, she looked round and saw his grey face. He was bareheaded. She hadn't seen his hat leave but it was scarcely to be expected that it shouldn't have. It was impossible to see anything of his expression although she did see his narrowed eyes. They were set with an incorrigible toughness. To beat him this storm would have first to kill him.

She forced up some of that same spirit in herself, lunged ahead and felt his hold on her hand loosen just a fraction. They were two-thirds of the way across. Ahead, dimly discernible through the waves of rain, were the stone fronts of buildings on the side-street and between two of them, too narrow for a car and perhaps built only to accommodate people on foot, or horsemen, lay the dark, water-filled cavern which was their destination.

She stumbled again but this time it was because she hadn't expected the kerb to be there. As before, he wrenched her back upright, gave a rough tug and literally dragged her on into the alleyway.

At once the storm abandoned them to press its assault upon the road behind them. He struggled through ankle-deep icy water seeking a doorway. There were none but a little distance ahead he did find a stone bin of some kind—for whatever purpose it had been constructed one could only guess, for it was very old and three-sided. He pushed her into this place, squeezed in beside her, released her blue fingers to pull down his coat-collar and say, 'It's not much farther.'

She heard him, which surprised her. All the wild howling was still around him. It just wasn't in their little stone bin which was man-high although barely wide enough for the pair of them to stand side by side.

She let her muscles loosen, leaning against him and the wet stones behind her. She raised her face out of the scratchy scarf and tasted salt-spray. When he moved at her side she looked in. He was rubbing his hands together. She wondered why he had no gloves.

'I'd never have made it except for you, back there in the road.'

He didn't comment but craned forward to study the sky from inside their cramped shelter. It seemed as though the heavens had fallen to rooftop level. Their alleyway, though, was actually running at cross-purposes to the force of the gale. It wasn't free of wind or driving rain but neither was it facing correctly to be a funnel for the raw violence in the street they'd just crossed.

He eased back, wiped his lips, his dripping forehead, turned and saw water on her chin and, using the same sodden white handkerchief, patted at her face. She smiled but it was an effort. Her face was cold as ice. He still had the handkerchief beneath her chin. When she smiled he turned her face to him, bent and kissed her. It was a shock. His lips were like ice.

'Come along,' he growled, grabbing at her hand again. She didn't want to leave their shelter so he pulled her away.

They had much less wind velocity to fight in their alley but the water pouring over their wellingtons was ice-cold. She shivered as he tugged her along, using her free hand to re-adjust the scratchy scarf. It made breathing possible.

They reached the rear of John Weldon's building and dimly discerned a light behind a warped shutter. It looked warmly inviting. He kept going, drawing her along with him.

She had thought her toes were numb before they had to begin stepping gingerly around debris being carried swiftly along in the ankle-deep water. He never slackened either his pace or his resolve. It almost annoyed her being dragged along like a recalcitrant child, but he probably wouldn't have allowed her to turn back if she'd wanted to.

She tried to catch sight of his profile and failed. He was hunched far over picking their way up-stream, paying her no heed whatsoever, evidently gauging her strength by the fact that she didn't lag against his hand.

Beyond Weldon's building there were several lower structures. Here, the wind caught them, making progress nearly as difficult as it had been out in the roadway.

He faltered, swaying with the wind rather than stubbornly opposing it, but he only slowed a bit, he never ceased moving ahead.

She was moving automatically by this time, muscles responding in dull sequence, nerves deadened by cold, by exhaustion, by an increasing sense of hopelessness.

She didn't like Joan Eaton, the iron-monger's wife, who was an inveterate gossip. She doubted that Mrs Eaton's stomach pains were anything more than storm-inspired tension and fear.

She resented her own high sense of duty and even thought uncharitably of her father who'd instilled into her this strong sense of duty.

As for the powerful hand which was, chain-like, dragging her without mercy through icy-water, punishing wind; and through darkness like the Pit, she mentally recoiled.

The kiss when she couldn't have resisted meant Will was no different from any other animal; he'd taken advantage of her. He'd do it again if the opportunity came.

She tried to fling free but his grip was like ice-cold iron. He turned, looked at her, slowed his pace slightly and began searching for another resting-place. She was staggering.

There were no recessed doorways and as far as he could see neither were there any more of those stone bins which had succoured them earlier. In fact there was nothing.

He hauled her up close, slid a powerful arm round her waist and began pushing onward again. She almost let him do it alone but conscience pricked her; this wasn't his obligation. He didn't have to go on; he didn't even have to be here with her. No one else had volunteered.

She tried to rally and keep up. He was

moving more slowly now, making that possible for her. Finally, he halted, held her against him with both arms, turned her head and jutted his chin towards the streaming windows of a house lying not more than a hundred or two yards onwards. He said nothing. He didn't have to make the attempt, she recognized the ironmonger's house.

She straightened up, turned and took an unsteady step. At once the strong arm was around her waist again. They covered the last few yards stumbling through icy-water, panting against the increasing wind like a pair of drunks.

She finally met a slippery pillar and clung to it. They were within ten feet of Frank Eaton's back door. They had made it!

CHAPTER SIX

The ironmonger's house was ten degrees too hot. At least that was what first struck Pat Brewster as she was helped to a small sofa in the cluttered parlour. Mrs Eaton was in bed, her husband told them as he offered both Pat and Will Forman a cup of scalding tea and suggested they shed their wellingtons and coats, which they did. He also said his wife was in great pain, but when Pat went in after a bit to examine the woman, she got the impression that there was less pain than terror. Nonetheless she was thorough, having suspected an infected appendix.

Her ultimate diagnosis was some form of mild food poisoning. At least Joan Eaton did not react unfavourably to any of the usual tests for appendicitis. She sent Frank Eaton to fetch some milk toast and suggested that he should give his wife no more tea. Then she returned to the parlour where Will was sitting in the suffocating heat with a scotch and water upraised. 'My fee,' he told her solemnly. 'Frank will bring you one in a moment.'

She didn't think she wanted one. In fact she did not care for scotch, but for that matter she'd never cared for the taste of any whisky.

She sank down in a chair, felt her drying hair, felt the heat which, in its excessive way, was nearly as unpleasant as the storm outside had been.

'What is it?' he asked, looking at her. 'Appendix?'

'Mild ptomaine, I'd guess.' She glanced at him, looked away and said, 'It's terribly hot in here—or is it me?'

'It's hot,' he assented and sipped his drink, looking at the guttering little stove through whose patch of discoloured glass in the door could be seen a sturdily persistent flame. 'Too cold or too hot—I suppose you'll remember this night for one or the other.'

'No,' she said slowly, 'I'll remember it for your heroism, Will.'

He gave an ugly, short laugh. 'Heroism? Just pushing through town to this place?' He shook his head and took another long pull from the glass in his hand. 'It took more courage to kiss you tonight, Pat, than it took to fight the beastly storm. I've been sitting here trying to decide whether it was the cold in the storm or the cold in your nature—your lips were like ice.'

She stiffened towards him. 'So were yours, so it must have been the storm.'

He turned mocking blue eyes. 'It's warm in here. We could try again.'

She rose as Frank Eaton came from the kitchen with a cup of what appeared to be tea for her, but the aroma was definitely different. Frank, a diffident, mild man smiled at her. 'Guaranteed,' he said, 'to stir up the blood again, Miss Brewster. And I must say how grateful I am that you came. I was at m'wits end, I don't mind saying.'

She accepted the tea, set it aside and asked what they'd had for supper. He mentioned several quite ordinary items, all tinned. She then asked if any of the food hadn't smelled quite right during preparation and Frank Eaton didn't know, for as he told her, he didn't have much to do in the kitchen. Then he asked if Pat was thinking of food poisoning. She nodded.

'It's probable, Mr Eaton.'

'Not the appendix?'

'No. At least if it is, your wife doesn't show any of the usual symptoms.'

Frank Eaton stepped to a little ladder-back chair and sat. He seemed somewhat relieved. 'If it'd been appendix, what could we've done?' he asked.

Pat was practical. 'Since it doesn't seem to be the appendix I don't think we need concern ourselves. I've brought several pills and if you'll see she gets nothing but milk—warm preferably—and takes the pills I'll leave with you, I think she'll be improved by morning.'

Eaton looked up quickly. 'You're not thinkin' of going back tonight? Miss Brewster, you can't make it.'

'We got here,' she said, stepping to the chair she'd vacated and seating herself again, without once looking at Will.

Eaton turned a troubled face to Forman. 'That's crazy,' he said.

Will, finishing his scotch and water, pleasantly nodded. His face looked slightly flushed from the heat but his eyes were as rock-steady as always. 'Without a doubt,' he said, agreeing with Frank Eaton. 'But Miss Brewster wouldn't want to leave her father alone on a night like this.'

She whirled on him but Will was looking at Frank Eaton, his profile to her. He didn't alter that position.

She kept control and very gradually relaxed. So *that* was what he thought of her; that she had the adolescent need for parental shelter. Or that she felt *she* was the sheltering one. It was ridiculous.

Frank Eaton said something she missed, but she heard Will Forman's answer; she was listening for it.

63

'Bad enough. I'd say it's nearly as bad as the one that struck on the sixth.'

Pat flared. *'Nearly* as bad! Mr Eaton it's every bit as bad.'

Eaton surprised her. He said, 'Not if Will says it isn't, Miss Brewster. It was him as got me home that night from the Coach an' Four. Not that I'd had too much, mind you, but I was a bit weakened by a bad cough you see.'

She looked at Forman. No one had said he'd done the same thing in that first storm he'd done for her tonight. He met her gaze looking sardonic.

'The Good Samaritan,' he said.

She rose to go to a mirror and try to do something with her hair. It was a hopeless undertaking. Her hair had a natural curl but the wind had made it into a natural tangle. She combed it, patted it down and glanced at her wristwatch. She then went back into the room where Joan Eaton lay and saw her patient eating warm toast soaked in milk. She smiled.

'Not very appetizing is it, Mrs Eaton?'

The ironmonger's wife was short, as he also was, and sturdy. She had coarse features but at one time, some fifteen or twenty years back, she'd been alluring in a definitely animal way. She was big-breasted, flat-bellied and with a flawless complexion even yet. She put aside the empty bowl and dropped back on the pillows.

'How did you ever make it?' she asked, rolling up her eyes as a drum-roll of distant thunder growled out of the ruptured heavens. 'It's worse'n the last one, it is.'

'Don't worry about it,' Pat suggested. 'Worrying isn't going to stop it, Mrs Eaton. How do you feel?'

'Better,' murmured the ill woman. She then proceeded to verify Pat's diagnosis of her trouble by saying, 'I told Frank one of the tins wasn't flat but was pushed out a bit.' She looked at Pat. 'The beans it was.'

'How much of it did you eat?'

'Thankfully only a mouthful or two, then Maggie Gibbon called t'say the storm'd peeled off their tool-shed roof an' when I come back Frank was clearing the table. The food was cold anyway... Besides I was scairt half t'death what with the wind and all. Had lost my appetite, I had.'

Pat was relieved. The nearest medical practitioner lived in the next village. Ordinarily, since he couldn't be expected to make a daily round of the villages in his area, the sick were driven over to him. Tonight that would have been impossible. She excused herself, went to the kitchen—which was a slatternly place, none too clean—and searched until she found the offending tin of beans. She examined it, wrinkled her nose and marvelled that Joan Eaton hadn't noticed the colour and smell.

When she returned to the parlour Frank Eaton had a glass of scotch in his hand. He and Will were quietly discussing what probable damage would come out of the storm.

She told them of the spoilt tin of beans. Frank said he didn't like the stuff and therefore hadn't eaten any. When she then told him that the telephone call might have prevented serious illness, he thought a bit and finally said with a crooked smile, 'I don't much care for Esau or his missus, but this time at least I'll say nothing about them exchangin' gossip on the telephone.'

Will was growing drowsy, she saw. She had noticed an inclination in that direction in herself. It was the heat in the house, which was a small residence even by Harlham standards, although the stove had obviously been designed for a more spacious place. She had often heard it said Americans required their houses to be extraordinarily warm, but whether this was so or not she personally didn't like a room to be warmer than sixty-five to sixty-eight degrees Fahrenheit.

She was uncertain whether to mention leaving or not. Will looked so comfortable, and he was dry now. Doubtless that scotch and water had done its soporific work as well. She sighed and sank into the chair. At once Frank Eaton pointed out that she hadn't touched her fortified cup of tea. She dutifully took a sip and struggled to keep from making a face. A little scotch would have been noticeable enough but there was a good deal more than that in the tea. She put the cup resolutely aside for the second time, this time firmly resolved to refuse if urged to drink again.

Joan called to her husband. He excused himself and went padding into the little cluttered bedroom in his flapping old slippers.

Pat went to a window to look out but there were sturdy wooden shutters over the glass so she went to the door and stood on tiptoe to see out through the tiny pane of glass there. All that was visible through streaked rows of scurrying rain was darkness. She didn't have to try hard to discern the sounds out there though, for the Eatons' house was without close neighbours and therefore caught every blast of wind on all sides.

'It hasn't let up,' said Will, from his slouched position in the chair. 'If you're set on getting back we'll go.'

She turned. He was looking up at her. The rain had nearly dried in his hair, which was more curly now than ever, and his rugged, strong features, relaxed by heat—inner and outer—were softened towards her. Without warning he said, 'Pat, you're very handsome. Even without your shoes, and I'll admit your feet are larger than I'd thought.' He grinned at the faint rush of colour under her cheeks. It was a malicious little grin. 'I've been thinking. Kiss me now and let's see whose lips are cold.'

She shot a look towards the bedroom door but Frank Eaton didn't appear to put an end to this personal conversation. Will pulled back his feet, straightened in the chair and mightily yawned.

'Forget it,' he said, sounding tired. 'But it's a vile trick—turning out something as beautiful as you are, then forgetting to put a heart and red blood in it.'

He stood up, ran a hand through his hair, stalked to the door and peered out. She moved warily away. Without turning he said, 'It's not going to let up until morning—if then.'

She went to her chair and sat down. There was a telephone across the room near the mirror, sitting on a small marble-topped table which was out of place in the parlour.

He turned, brought her wellingtons and stepped back to get his own and yawned again. 'Maybe we'd better leave,' he said. 'I'll fall asleep in another few minutes.'

She felt sorry for him. He moved as easily as always but there was no disguising the fact that he was tired. She said, 'You can't have got much rest last night.'

He sank down to put on his wellingtons without answering. His face had a brooding look to it, the eyes were hidden from her her but the long, full lips were flattened with an expression of dogged resolve.

'Will, we can stay if you think we ought to.'

'No. You'll want to get back to your Father, Pat. We'll go.'

She bit back a short comment, waited a moment then said, 'He'll be quite all right. He doesn't need me.'

He went right on pulling on his wellingtons. '*He* doesn't need you, right enough, but *you* need *him*.' He looked at her. 'Put your wellingtons on.'

Before she could speak he rose, flexed his arms, plunged both hands into his trouser pockets and went across to meet Frank Eaton who was emerging from the bedroom.

'We'll be getting back,' he told the ironmonger. 'Pat'll probably be needed elsewhere anyway.'

Eaton renewed his earlier protests. He even pointed to a dilapidated sofa saying it opened out into a bed. Pat, watching Will, saw he was not going to budge. She bent and pulled on her wellingtons then rose to get her coat. Just for a moment she felt light-headed, then that passed and she blamed the tea.

Outside, a great wave of raw fury broke over the top of the house, making it appear for a moment the roof would be carried away. Joan squeaked from within the bedroom and Frank ran to comfort her.

CHAPTER SEVEN

The wind was less but the rain had increased considerably. The alleyway which they proceeded to pass down again, promptly filled their wellingtons once more with icy water.

It shocked Will fully awake with its bone-chill. Frank Eaton had made the offer of a hat but since his head was smaller than Will's the offer had been declined on the grounds the too-small hat wouldn't have lasted fifty yards anyway, which was true enough, for although the wind had noticeably lessened it most certainly had not ceased.

Rain didn't come in drops it came in sheets of water at close-spaced intervals. If one dared one could look up and see those great sheets of water moving ahead. The wind had risen somewhat; it was still audible overhead, but higher up now, making a great booming sound as it roared unobstructed across the countryside.

They got as far as the man-high old

stone bin and crowded in again. Pat's strength had returned after the respite at Frank Eaton's place, but she had an uneasy feeling she would have to conserve it to reach home again. Of course the icy rain kept her alert, but it also made her feel chilled to the knees.

Will rubbed the hand he was holding and smiled at her. She started to smile back, then didn't; this was the very spot he'd kissed her. She gently tugged to free the hand he'd rubbed warmth into. He released it, looking at her a moment, stepped ahead to peer outwards, eased back and shook his head. Nothing had changed out there.

She noticed something he didn't see. The water in their little alleyway was growing swifter and deeper. She tugged at Will to point this out. He took her hand and started onward again. Of course there was no danger from the water because their alley was open at both ends, but it was difficult to walk through when it had such a violent current, and it also increased the sensation of freezing.

They reached the end of the alley without incident. The wind was still roaring up through the unobstructed roadway but its lower-down force seemed less. They still had to fight for every yard they traversed and reaching the far side spent Pat's strength. She slumped when he pulled her over the kerb, held out both hands to keep from falling, and would have fallen anyway except that he jumped back and somehow got tight hold of her. She never afterwards understood how he managed, but he half dragged, half carried her the last twenty feet.

She was perfectly rational except for a recurrence of that light-headedness she'd briefly noticed back at the Eaton home. But her legs and arms weighed a ton. It was an effort, when he eased her down in a sitting position, just to get both hands into her lap. It was ridiculous. She'd expected to be spent but not thoroughly exhausted like this.

He knelt to shield her with his body. His face was screwed into an expression of frank anxiety. She tried to smile but of course the scratchy scarf hid most of her face. She wanted to reach forth and touch him to let him know she'd be all right, but something told her she *wasn't* all right even before she found that raising the hand took an almost superhuman effort on her part, and stopped trying.

He shouted something. Wind tore the words away before he'd got them out. A veritable wave of water hit them. He twisted from the waist, studied the black night, the distance to the corner where they could rest once more, and looked at her again. This time she saw his eyes widen. He reached up very slowly, put a hand on her shoulder and removed it.

That was when she saw the blood.

At first she thought he'd been injured, then the expression in his eyes and a sudden belated fierce ache in the back of her head told it wasn't Will at all, it was *she* who'd been injured.

She blinked, tried to raise a hand which he caught and pushed down again. She had no recollection of any pain until this moment. Even then it wasn't sharp the way pain from a wound should be. She never did, in fact, completely understand why this happened as it did.

With the ache though, the heaviness departed from her legs and arms. She reached for him and clung to the soggy coat. She tried to say they should get along. He either caught her thought or decided they'd rested long enough; he took both her hands, raised up slowly bringing her up with him, and when she was caught by a savage gust of water he turned her with both arms, hooked a powerful grip around her waist and let the force of the storm carry them all the way to the corner and around it. There, with much less wind although the rain never lessened in its savage lashing, he held her against a stone wall, fished for his sodden white handkerchief and deftly wiped the back of her head where the ache lay. She saw the handkerchief. It was scarlet, watered blood dripped from it. She finally raised a hand to explore the injury. She'd evidently been struck from behind by some flying object, perhaps one of the slates off a roof.

It was baffling though; she had no recollection of the blow and there'd been no immediate pain. She pushed his hand away, turned to gauge the distance to her father's house and took a forward step. This time her legs were willing. Weak but willing. He kept hold of her hand and moved close beside her ready in an instant to grab.

They covered a dozen yards, then he pointed to the same recessed doorway they'd used on their way out. She stumbled here, neglecting to recall the stone step. He eased her back as far as the opening allowed, placed himself in front of her again, and everything except the roar was shut out.

She tugged down the scarf, felt the back of her head and noticed for the first time her hat was gone. He grimly smiled. 'You look a fright,' he said. She smiled back.

'I didn't feel it happen.'

'You stumbled,' he shouted. 'That's when I thought something had happened. But I didn't see the blood until I had pulled you across the road.'

'Will, there's very little sensation of pain. Is it bad?'

She turned his face, he bent close in the gloom then drew back. 'You'll live,' he shouted. 'But we'd better make it the rest of the way. It's bleeding a bit.'

She thought most of the flow was probably rainwater but didn't say so. It was difficult to shout loudly enough to be heard and she was beginning to have a corker of a headache.

Her father's house was close by, thankfully, for the wind now swung round and began sweeping up in a fresh direction. This seemed to presage something, perhaps a diminution, or possibly only a change in the violence. One thing it did was make the walking more difficult. Will slid an arm around her and used his body as much as possible to shield her.

Once half a window shutter hurtled past them torn from a house across the way. There was also a sound of tinkling glass over there. Doubtless other noises were also being made as the storm assaulted Harlham from a fresh direction, but neither Pat nor Will made any point of detecting them.

A face appeared at a ground-floor window. They only glimpsed it for a moment between waves of downpour. It looked out at them utterly flabbergasted, as though it had seen ghosts, then they were past, the darkness engulfed them and, as before, they might have been the only two people on earth.

She began to weaken again with her father's threshold in full view. She rallied, encouraged by the sight of it and clung to his arm until she reached the door, then sagged against the outer wall as Will stepped ahead to reach for the latch. The light-headedness was returning.

She knew she was inside and seated by

the warmth by the sudden cessation of tumult. She also felt her father's quick, probing hands and recognized them as well. When he first saw the discoloured back of her head, dress and coat, he'd uttered a sharp cry. She'd also heard that.

She let her eyes close. Just not having to battle for every step, for each breath, was enormous relief.

It was the dull ache that forced her to look up, to open her eyes and take quick stock of things. She'd been asleep but it took a gradual realization of this to bring her upright off the sofa where they'd put her under a blanket. The fireplace danced with little red flames, her father was seated in his chair drinking something amber from a glass, and across from him Will Forman sat, his hair and clothing completely dry, which gave her some clue as to how long she'd slept.

Will softly shook his head at her. 'Lie back. Go back to sleep.'

Will's words gave her father a slight start where he sat. She smiled at him. He asked how she felt. She paused to take stock then said, 'Not bad.' They'd put a small bandage on the back of her head where the slate had struck and although there was swelling there as well as a lingering vestige of that dull headache, she actually felt rather well, considering all she'd been through.

She let herself lie back. It was sheerest luxury being here like this, warmly snug in a room with companions, heat from the fireplace.... She suddenly stiffened beneath her blanket. She wasn't wearing the soggy dress. In fact she wasn't wearing any dress at all. She was wrapped in her robe beneath the cover, her feet and legs bare.

Only for a moment did she feel chagrin. Common sense told her they couldn't have left her in the soaked, blood-stained dress anyway. She half smiled at her own near panic. What a frightful night for false modesty.

They were speaking, Will's voice deeper than her father's voice, his words slowly measured as though he were rationing them. The storm, he was saying, seemed to be turning less into a gale and more into a squall. She dreamily wondered if perhaps the difference weren't a matter of semantics. Then she heard Will explaining that the wind was breaking up, was coming in upon Harlham from all directions, creating shrieking tumult but actually spending its violence against itself.

She heard her father say, 'I hope that means an end to it.'

'A beginning to the end at least,' Will rejoined, and she heard his chair squeak as he rose. 'I'll go to look in on them.'

She felt numbness coming, drowsiness returning. Will was a strong man, she thought hazily. If strength were all a girl needed... *Look in on them?* Her eyes popped wide open. *Look in on whom?* She raised her head slightly to watch Will stride silently across the room on his way.

She said, 'Will...?'

He turned near the foot of the couch. 'Thought you were asleep.'

'Who are you going to look in on?'

He stood above her gazing down, his face slack and dark-ringed but with no sign of weakening resolve in it. 'Gordon Johnson,' he said, 'and that girl called Everett from the upper end of town.'

'They're—here—in this house?'

Her father arose a trifle stiffly and came across to the sofa. 'I called over to Eatons', Pat, but you and Will had already gone. Gordon came along only a short while after you'd left. He barely managed to get here.

80

The girl didn't manage it but one of the neighbours called and Will went down and got her.'

'Are they injured?' she asked.

'Johnson's arm is broken in two places,' said Will. 'The girl delivered twenty minutes after we got her into your bed.'

'She—*what!*'

Will smiled at her incredulity but old Brewster was as unsmiling as a judge. He'd evidently not yet recovered from the shock himself.

Pat sat straight up. A throb of pain made itself felt in the back of her head from the effort. She stared at Will. 'You—delivered her baby, Will?'

'Someone had to, Pat. You weren't in any shape to. Actually there wasn't much to it. I'd never been around when it'd happened before but I suppose, everything being normal, anyone could have done it.'

Her father said, 'I read from one of your medical books while Will officiated.' Old Brewster's eyes looked sunken with exhaustion. 'A bit harrowing. Of course the lights went out half-way through and we finished by candlelight.'

Until that moment although she'd noticed

there was no light in the warm parlour, she hadn't noticed the fireplace gave the only illumination. She just hadn't thought about it. She reached to heave aside the cover and rise. Her father moved to intercede but Will shook his head.

'You can't stop her,' he said, and stood watching, making no move to help at all.

CHAPTER EIGHT

Gordon Johnson had been put in her father's room. He was dozing when she entered followed by her father and Will Forman. He blinked, yawned, moved slightly and winced.

They had made a competent enough bandage. It was rough, unprofessional and bulky but Mr Johnson seemed in no pain and when she bent to make an examination he told her the arm wasn't troubling him. Her private thought was that just being totally motionless, the chances were excellent that it wouldn't bother him, but that did not necessarily imply the bones had been properly set. She didn't say anything like this. In fact she said nothing at all.

Johnson explained how it'd happened. 'Stepped out to have a look about at the precise moment a great tree limb was torn from an oak. The thing struck me as I was trying to jump clear. Like a juggernaut it was. I knew of course oak was a very tight-grained heavy wood but I'd no idea it was *that* heavy. The thing was like solid iron. It knocked me flat. If it had struck at a different angle it would have pinned me down by the chest.'

She thought that if the big limb had caught Johnson across the chest he'd have been dead by now. 'I'll be back after a while,' she said. 'Can we bring you something hot?'

The retired solicitor shook his head, 'No, thank you. I'm chagrined, actually, to be putting you to all this inconvenience. Bad enough even to trouble you, but this is your father's bedroom.'

Old Brewster said, 'I couldn't sleep anyway, tonight, but, if I'd felt like it, believe me there are other beds.'

They left Gordon Johnson. In the hallway with nothing but the overhead roof between them and the storm they could

83

distinctly hear clamour. If the pounding was less the rain certainly didn't sound much abated.

The Everett girl, whose first name was Catherine, had two candles, one on a nightstand on either side of the bed. She wasn't a very large girl but in Pat's bed she looked actually very childlike. Her eyes were huge and troubled, her face was waxen. She eyed the three of them with grave doubt but Pat noticed one thing straight-away; whenever she thought she was unobserved she followed Will Forman wherever he moved with those large, dark eyes.

The baby was wrinkled and red with lank dark hair and fat arms and fists. He made small noises but did not cry. Will held the girl's hand a moment, then he and old Brewster went out into the hall. Pat sat on the edge of the bed. She'd delivered babies before and the actual delivery was only a prelude to all that came afterwards. She talked with the girl soothingly and discovered something that was holding Catherine Everett in deep dread. Her husband was a seaman. She had last heard of him in the North Sea. If this storm had come from out there...

Pat was reassuring. 'Will Forman was a seaman too, and he said something earlier about the storm probably originating not too far from our coasts, so if your husband isn't near Britain I should imagine he's safer than you and I are.'

It wasn't necessarily true but Pat wasn't too concerned with the logic; she wanted the girl to rest as best she could. She'd had a harrowing enough experience this night. They all had.

'If something has happened to him,' said Catherine Everett, 'I don't know what I'll do—what *we'll* do. He told me before he went away he would bring his son something.' The dark-ringed large eyes softened a little. 'He knew it would be a son.'

Pat smiled. He'd been right. Above them the roof creaked, the wind pounced, the rain hammered wildly. There was a small room off the kitchen, a sort of lean-to used by previous owners, no doubt, as a servant's quarters. It might have been better to put the girl there. There was a bed and she'd have been less likely to hear the tumult outside.

Pat lay a hand on Catherine's slight arm. 'Didn't you know before the storm?' she asked, and saw at once by the look in the child-bride's eyes that not only hadn't Catherine known, she hadn't been strong enough to resist panic when it had finally begun to happen.

'I tried to get up here,' she said, looking at Pat with frightened eyes as she re-lived her terrible experience. 'I tried—but the storm—it would push me back. I even tried to reach the home of a neighbour but there was no one at home.'

'How did Mr Forman find you?'

'I don't know. One minute I was huddling in a doorway, the next moment he was there looking like a giant. I—fainted. He told me that.'

'He carried you here?'

'Yes. He and your father put me to bed—then the baby started coming...'

Pat smoothed back the girl's tumbled hair. 'It's all right now, Catherine. Everything is fine. Sleep if you can. I'll be back after a bit with some breakfast. Is there anything I can get you meanwhile?'

The large brown eyes softened towards Pat. 'No thank you... He was positively heroic, Miss Brewster.'

She returned to the hallway. Her father and Will were in Gordon Johnson's room talking with the injured solicitor. Johnson's voice sounded strong; it also sounded loud and a little garrulous. She thought she knew what medication Will and her father had prescribed as she stepped to the doorway.

Will saw her, turned and raised his brows. She told them the girl was fine; still recovering from her terror of the storm and her more recent physical ordeal, but otherwise quite well.

Gordon Johnson said. 'I was just saying, that in my lifetime I've survived war, epidemics, financial reverses, illnesses, always with the thought that some day I'd be able to retire to the country and spend the remaining years of my life pottering about. Then damned if I don't nearly get killed there. Now that's the irony of a man's destiny I'd say, Miss Brewster, wouldn't you also say it was?'

She nodded, not convinced by Mr Johnson's arguments for the simple reason that accidents can occur anywhere at any time, but unwilling to become involved in a long discussion on human destiny either.

'I'll get some things to re-set the arm,'

she said, and left them.

For a moment Gordon Johnson peered at the doorway where she'd been, then looked at old Brewster and Will Forman. 'Re-set the arm?' he muttered. 'Confound it what does she mean—re-set the arm? I thought once a broken limb was set it wasn't to be fussed over until the bones knit again.'

Brewster had no knowledge of such things. Even though he'd heard his daughter explain about broken bones and minor illnesses for several years, because he lacked interest he'd made no attempt to pick any of it up. He looked dubiously at the cast. His expression made Will smile. The cast was crude looking. He said, 'She's right, Mr Johnson.'

Brewster looked relieved. 'Maybe a dram of whisky would help,' he said, and turned to leave. Neither Will nor Gordon Johnson made a move to stop him but after they'd heard him descending the stairs Johnson peered at Will in the candlelight.

'Bad out?'

'Pretty bad.'

'Letting up any yet?'

Will couldn't say with any degree of certainty, so he only said the wind had changed course and the rain was increasing.

Johnson turned glum. 'There'll be damage this time; we'll be lucky if it's only a few roofs torn loose.' He considered Will's face a moment then said, 'That little girl in the other room—didn't she say her husband was a seaman?'

Will nodded, stepped to a shuttered window and strove to see out through a crack. It was too dark to see much.

'For her sake,' growled Johnson, 'I hope he's in the Pacific or the Mediterranean. The North Sea'll have its tragedies this night.'

Will returned to the chair he'd vacated saying nothing. He was beginning to drag a little as he moved, his eyes were sinking into his head. He'd fought the storm twice, hadn't had any rest since the night before, and regardless of stamina and strength, was nearing the end of his reserves.

When Pat returned she had everything required for a proper splint but Gordon Johnson resisted. As a great gust of wind tore over the house, making Pat jump, he demanded to be told why the splint he was wearing wasn't adequate.

Pat was diplomatic. 'I get paid for doing

this, Mr Johnson. I'm provided with all the things to do it with. You wouldn't want to see me done out of my job, would you?'

Johnson looked sullen as he said, 'Forman did a first rate job, you know. He's set his share of broken arms—legs too—he told me.'

She turned. Will was gazing detachedly at them. 'You've done this before?' she asked.

'My share of times, yes.'

'I didn't know you were—'

'It doesn't matter, really. I'm sure your training makes you far superior.' Will rose as her father came puffing up the stairs with two glasses, one in each hand. He accepted one glass, thanked old Brewster, looked at Pat and said, 'Go ahead—re-bandage it. I'm not thin-skinned.' He then took a deep drink and kept watching her almost sardonically, almost as though he knew something she didn't know.

Gordon Johnson also got his tot of whisky. It seemed to make him less reluctant. When Pat put the arm out and started removing the improvised bandage she noticed something; Will's wrapping didn't go round and round the splinted arm. It instead ran diagonally so that one layer lay on a sloping angle while the next layer ran upwards giving a laminated effect.

She'd never seen bandaging like that before. Also, the splints were parts of one of her father's cigar boxes, and the bones had been pulled out then socketed together perfectly. It was as professional a job as she'd ever seen.

She turned to speak. Only her father was in the room with Brewster. Will was gone. She said nothing and went to work with the fresh bandaging. Johnson made a face once or twice and commented on the fact that plaster-of-Paris was used in most of the bone-sets he'd ever seen.

She didn't explain about that either although she had a valid reason for what she was doing: The arm would have to be re-examined and X-rayed at the cottage hospital as soon as it was possible to get over there, when the permanent cast would be applied.

Johnson's ordeal had actually been very debilitating, but he'd been recuperating now for several hours. Having a strong constitution too, helped. And doubtless the splint prevented him from experiencing much physical pain while his host's scotch also contributed to his general overall well-being.

He protested about keeping old Brewster's bedroom and insisted upon being permitted to go downstairs. Pat had no objection, once the arm was re-wrapped. Her father went down with Johnson. They both had expected to find Will Forman down there sitting by the fire but he didn't come along until a short while after they'd got comfortable. He'd been upstairs with the Everett girl. He'd left only when Pat had come into the room.

He was still nursing that whisky old Brewster had got him. Fortunately it was British custom to eschew the use of ice, therefore, as Will sank into a chair and finished off what was left, he found nothing wrong with a tepid drink.

Gordon Johnson said the storm must be dying because he could hear nothing. Brewster explained why that was—downstairs one heard practically nothing of what was happening out-of-doors.

Johnson rose, crossed to a shuttered window and tried to see out. He ended up by the front door. While he was doing this Pat's father told Will it was nearly dawn, and that in his experience even the worst storms tended to lessen somewhat at daybreak.

Will said nothing but he politely nodded, watched Johnson return, shoved out his legs and slouched in tired relaxation.

It had been a difficult night. Of course it wasn't over, but none of them sitting there by the fire really expected much more to happen.

'Act of God,' said Johnson, staring broodingly into the fire. He'd evidently recalled the gist of an earlier conversation. 'Did you hear what Sloat said?'

They'd heard. They would have said something too, no doubt, but Pat came downstairs distracting them. She stood briefly limned in golden candlelight in the hall, then came towards them smiling. Will's eyes broodingly held on her all the way across the room. Her father saw that look and fidgeted where he sat. But then the candlelight was very poor so he may possibly have misread Will's expression.

CHAPTER NINE

The telephone rang when they were having their respite by the fireplace. Will had visibly to struggle even to lift his head to listen. Pat went to answer it and although none of the men in the parlour could very clearly make out the one-sided conversation they all showed in their faces they expected this to be a distress call from someone.

It wasn't. When Pat returned she informed them the telephone people were making routine checks as to the condition of everyone. They were also passing on the information that there'd been widespread flooding throughout Harlham and that the Royal Engineers were on their way.

Gordon Johnson cocked an eyebrow. 'On their way? What time is it? Where've they been all night, I'd like to know. It's almost morning; will be in another hour or two although I doubt that one'd know it except for the clocks.'

Pat asked Will to lend a hand in the

kitchen making breakfast for them all but particularly for Catherine Everett. Brewster and Johnson exchanged a significant look but neither commented on the fact that anyone—almost anyone at any rate—could have got breakfast for five people, without an assistant.

Will dutifully left the older men and followed Pat through the house. They had to light candles which fortunately were not in short supply, and when Pat bent to stir up some life in the stove she sent Will into the pantry for some tinned things. He returned laden, set the tins on a small table and found her standing near the stove facing him.

'I don't want you to think I re-bandaged Mr Johnson's arm or made some minor re-arrangements with Catherine to spite you, Will.'

'The idea hadn't crossed my mind,' he said, straightening up from the little table between them. 'It's your job. I only filled in until you got round to it.'

'And, I wanted to tell you I'm awfully grateful. You've been...' she groped for the right word, recalled Catherine's description and used it before thinking, 'heroic tonight.'

He wrinkled his brow a little. 'Hardly heroic,' he said dryly. 'Useful, handy, functional, but hardly heroic.'

She accepted the rebuff, watched him glance at the tins, then over at the stove and slowly turned to start things cooking. She knew she'd failed. Her intention had been to tell him privately how deeply she appreciated all he'd done. How she'd felt blessed having him to help.

She'd used a word he seemed sceptical of and that had put them back where they'd been earlier—at dagger-point.

He came over to watch, saying, 'How's the headache?'

She had to stop and think. It was gone. Evidently it had been gone some time. She put a hand to the back of her head to feel the little bandage and the lump. Both were very much still in evidence but otherwise there were no lasting after-effects.

'Gone,' she said, looking at him.

He nodded. They weren't more than three feet apart. 'You look a lot better. For a while there you seemed a little groggy.'

'Tired,' she said, turning back to her work at the stove. 'Of course that was all quite difficult, out there tonight, but I'd always felt sure my personal stamina was greater than that.'

'It was adequate,' he assured her, 'until that slate or whatever it was clouted you.'

She looked up again. 'That was the oddest thing, Will. I felt nothing. I didn't even know I'd been struck. It just seemed all my strength deserted me.'

He said he knew the sensation and reached to put the kettle on to boil. Their shoulders touched. It was as though something electric had brushed against them. She moved slightly to her left to avoid a repetition and he drew back the arm. Neither looked at the other. He broke the odd silence by saying Catherine Everett's tiny son had picked a disastrous night to make his appearance.

It was an easy thing to say; the kind of comment a woman might find convenient at a time like this, but not many men would have been so facile. She appreciated what he'd tried to do and agreed with him. She also said it was a sturdy little boy. Since neither of them knew Catherine Everett's husband they'd exhausted that topic.

He then made a remark that swept away all her previous gratitude to him for being diplomatic. He said, 'Pat, I'm not saying any man is much different from any other man because by instinct and chemistry they are pretty much the same. But I *will* say two men can act totally differently from one another.'

She knew at once what he was driving at and said without looking round, 'I'm surprised my father should be so confiding.'

'He wasn't all that confiding, but then I didn't descend in the last rain either.'

'I'm grateful for your interest, but could we discuss something else?'

'Sure,' he said gruffly. 'The storm. It's still out there, unquestionably there's been damage, doubtless it will continue for a while yet, and we are probably as safe as anyone can be. All right, that sums it all up. What's left to say?'

She kept her face lowered and averted. The rings under her eyes lent her face a haunted, melancholy expression which was very attractive. She'd combed her hair upstairs, had put on a fresh dress too. She moved mechanically, as though he'd somehow hurt her and for a while she'd function on instinct until the pain passed.

He watched her. Even when a particularly savage gust of wind-driven rain struck the side of the house he did not look away. She did; she flinched and looked round. Of course there was nothing to see. There was another house to break the brunt of that stunning force anyway but her nerves were on edge.

'Encore,' he growled at her, referring to the sudden fury outside.

She kept looking at him. 'Please, Will...' She went back to her cooking.

He seemed about to capitulate, to honour her plea. Then he yanked out a chair, put a foot upon it and leaned upon the upraised leg as he said savagely, 'Do you think it's healthy, what you're doing, Pat? Don't you suppose people have heard about your luckless love affair? Well, the world hasn't ended, has it? There are other men. Everything passes—even this blasted storm. You know what people will do when this is past; they'll clean up the mess and start living all over again. You've failed at it, Pat, and your personal storm isn't even half as important nor critical.'

She swung on him. 'How can you say that? How do you know what my personal storm was like?'

'Because I've been there, too,' he shot back at her. 'Do you think you're the only

99

person on earth who's fallen deeply in love, and had the earth pulled out from under them? Well, duck, you're not, and that's a damned fact.'

She was breathing hard. It wasn't easy controlling temper when one's nerves were already shredded. Still, he'd definitely shocked her with his personal revelation. She stood stiffly eyeing him for a while, until some of the starch went out, then she started to speak, changed her mind, half turned back towards the stove and said, 'I'm sorry, Will.'

'So am I,' he said, his voice roughened. 'Do you want to know what happened? She died. Now in your case you've got a man to hate for what he did to you. What have *I* got? Nothing tangible at all. I was told the Lord giveth and He taketh away. Well, that's no consolation, Pat. That's no answer at all.'

She said, her back to him. 'Is there any answer, Will?'

'Yes, there's an answer, but you don't find it at once. It's the obvious one. She is gone and I'm still here; life doesn't stop for me although I would have welcomed death the year after she died. But life doesn't stop, so I go on living it. And what applies in my case also applies in yours.'

She said softly, 'The water is boiling.'

She got a tray to take upstairs. When he offered to carry it she declined on the grounds there were things she could do better up there alone. He didn't question that. When she returned a little later he'd set the kitchen table, made the tea and dished up the food.

She told him he was very gifted and smiled. 'Just get 'em in here,' he growled, turning away from her.

It was like a slap in the face. She stood without moving for a moment, colour climbing into her face, then she briskly moved around the table, reached and swung him half around.

'If you want to sulk,' she told him furiously, 'don't do it here!'

He was surprised, there was no denying that, but he wasn't just surprised, he was also stung. 'Sulk? Sulk about what? Because you're a disappointment as a woman—a dead fish? Pat, I couldn't sulk about that, I could only feel sorry for you because you'd just not be much of a woman.'

'Would you be an authority?' she demanded.

101

He nodded, looking sulphurously down into her tilted face. 'Damned right I'd know, Pat, because once, a long way from Harlham, I knew a real woman. She made me an authority on womankind the first year I knew her.'

'And you're convinced she was the only one.'

'I'm convinced now,' he told her flatly. 'I wasn't sure until tonight. I've got the storm to thank for that.'

'Thank you,' she icily said, turned and marched from the room.

He didn't go after her. He went to the sink for a glass of water, drank it and turned as Gordon Johnson and Pat's father came in to have their breakfast. He kept watching the doorway but Pat did not return.

Brewster took a place at the head of the little table waving Johnson and Will Forman to chairs. The solicitor sat straightaway, obviously ravenous, but Will kept waiting for the door to open. It never did.

'Sit, boy, sit,' growled Johnson. 'Surely after all your heroics tonight you're hungry.'

'You know what you can do with that

kind of "Heroic" talk don't you?' shot back Will Forman, looking coldly at the older man.

Johnson was shocked at the venom in Forman's face and tone. 'Sorry,' he said, when he recovered from surprise. 'Really didn't mean anything, you know...'

Old Brewster looked up annoyedly. 'Sit down, Will; it's that confounded storm. Come along now.'

But Will walked out into the parlour evidently unable to shake off his mood of strong resentment and irritation. Pat wasn't out there which was doubtless just as well.

The fire had been freshly fed, indicating that Pat *had* been there. He guessed she'd be upstairs with the Everett girl, turned and went to the door to look out.

The storm was definitely diminishing. It was still fierce out there, but the wind was gusty now, had lost a good deal of its momentum and had little ragged interludes between each burst.

The rain was coming with less force now. It was slower and softer, almost like a heavy springtime downpour. There was as yet no sign of the dawn but there shortly would be. He turned when someone spoke.

103

It was Pat across the entry hall standing on the last step before completing her return from upstairs.

She had one hand lightly lying upon the ancient rail, the other hand at her side. In candlelight her face was half shadowed and made girlish, the chin round, the heavy lips not as astringently held as they usually were, the soft glow of her dark eyes quietly radiant and virginal.

He blew out a ragged breath and said, 'It's letting up a bit. I'll be moving along shortly.'

'Have you had breakfast?'

'Not hungry,' he said, staring at her.

'You've got to eat, Will.'

'Later.'

They stood a moment in quiet thought. She did not drop her eyes before his stare. She knew how she looked in his eyes; she'd seen that identical expression on other masculine faces before her love affair and afterwards. It didn't repel her; it was a natural thing. But that's as far as it would ever go.

'At least,' she finally said, stepping down off the step, 'we've got to know each other tonight, Will.'

'That we have,' he agreed bitterly. 'That

we have, Pat. I suppose one could say the storm wasn't *all* bad.'

She ignored his implication. 'And whether you like it or not, Catherine Everett and I think you were heroic.'

He crookedly smiled. 'I don't want to fight any more, Pat. Heroic it is. As for the other—I'm sorry I flared out at you.'

She couldn't answer this so readily so she simply inclined her head a little, moved towards the archway leading towards the dining-room and the kitchen beyond.

'Please come and eat something, Will.'

She did an unexpected thing; she held out a hand to him. He didn't take it. He wasn't a child to be soothed and led to the breakfast table. He *did* go with her though.

CHAPTER TEN

An hour before dawn John Weldon telephoned to tell Will his cellar was flooding. Weldon laughed about it. His rooms were upstairs above the pub so he had very little to fear. He'd just been wondering how others were making out, he said, and stated surprise that the telephones were still working.

As far as they knew the flooding was now Harlham's greatest peril for the wind was steadily diminishing. It had blown madly for something like eight hours, hadn't been able to level the town and was now spent which left the rain as the primary enemy.

Rain didn't often terrify people. Wind did; by its very nature, wild and physically forceful and noisy, wind struck some deep-down primitive chord. And yet the rain was more imminently likely to bring the village to ruin. Regardless of how ancient and time-tested the buildings were, their foundations were set in the ground, and water softened, weakened the earth under those footings. Ordinarily it would doubtless have remained imprisoned between high kerbings which was the way the town had been planned—so that roads also served as community drains—but there were definite limitations too; none of the roadways had been engineered to carry off veritable rivers of water.

Old Brewster's house had a cellar. In fact if there were many homes in Harlham that didn't possess cellars no one at the

Brewster place knew anything about them.

Gordon Johnson telephoned his house-keeper and told her to have the gardener stand by with buckets or whatever he could improvise to battle flooding in the cellar. He also told her he wouldn't be able to get back until the storm had let up a bit more.

The sound of tons of water ominously filling the street yonder, crashing around corners, lapping against stone buildings, replaced the sound of a gradually dying wind. It was difficult to determine which was the more frightening sound. One thing was certain; neither sound had any reassurance to it at all.

Will went to the head of the back steps with Pat's father to hold aloft a candle and peer down. Water was trickling in from several places. Most noticeably it ran in round a little iron-barred window down there. Will descended to assess the peril.

He found some rags and, using a screwdriver he found upon an old work-bench, caulked round the window. It didn't stop the water but it reduced it considerably. He told old Brewster that if the water didn't find another way in he thought the storm would have passed

107

before any appreciable amount of water got in.

Paul Brewster was concerned for Will's shop and offered to brave the flood to go down there with him. Will said there was no need. His building had no cellar. It was one of the few relatively modern buildings in Harlham. If the wind died, then actually the rain couldn't harm him. Anyway, he ruefully said as they began climbing up out of the cellar, whatever damage had been done, had been done, had been accomplished hours ago; going down there now wasn't going to change any thing.

Gordon Johnson was agitatedly awaiting them at the top of the stairs. 'She got a call,' he blurted at them. 'She's going out.'

Will didn't wait for particulars but strode swiftly through to the little hall where a candle smokily sputtered. Pat had her coat and hat on, she was pulling on her wellingtons when he burst upon her. She looked calmly up at him.

'One of the Sloat children was struck by a falling timber.'

He swore. The Sloat farm was miles out. 'You can't possibly get out there, Pat. It's three miles to the farm and another—'

'I won't have to go so far. Jeremy's wife called to say he'd started for town with the child on his tractor. She was crying but she said Jeremy had told her if anything could get through...'

'Yes, I can imagine,' he interrupted. 'If anything can get the job done it'll be his tractor. Then why go out? Why not just wait?'

'Because if he can't come all the way I'll need to be where I can reach him.'

Will could plainly see the determination. He started to remonstrate but set his jaw in a dogged manner, turned and reached for his own coat and wellingtons. 'Get me a hat,' he growled at her.

She sat with one wellington on, the other in her hand. 'Will, you're tired.'

'So are you.'

'But this is my job—my duty.'

'What difference will that make if you cave in half way along? Harlham doesn't need any dead heroines—drowned in a ridiculous flood.'

'I'll manage, Will.'

'You wouldn't even get half-way there. Pat. Now find me a decent hat.' He stood up, stamping his feet in their wellingtons.

'Don't just sit there, girl—the hat confound it!'

She rose but instead of moving she said, 'I won't let you do it. You've already done much more than—'

'You can't stop me. Now will you get that hat?' When she wavered and he saw this he said, 'Pat, what of Catherine upstairs and the baby? They certainly need you a lot more than I do, or than Sloat does. At least you can help here at home, and I can't.'

It wasn't the truth. She knew she'd been trained and at least in that regard what he'd said might have been true, but she also knew something else from the way he'd set Johnson's arm and had delivered Catherine's child. Somewhere, somehow, he'd learnt how to care for the injured and the ill.

But it was also very clear from the look on his face that he wasn't going to permit her to leave the house. Furthermore, he was right. She couldn't stop him from going out.

'The hat,' he said quietly, watching emotions come and go across her features. 'Or shall we stand here staring each other down until Sloat's drowned out there?'

She turned to find her father and get him a hat. While he stood buttoning his coat Gordon Johnson came in from the kitchen. The solicitor looked Will up and down and gave his leonine head a sharp wag.

'When will it end?' he growled, as though the storm were some human enemy. 'Where the devil are those Royal Engineers?'

Pat returned with her father who was carrying two hats, one of felt and the other of some coarse-grained tweed material. The latter was a cap which Will took. It fitted him tightly but adequately. As he was adjusting it the others stood funereally around saying nothing and watching. He smiled at the two older men. 'You may never get this cap back,' he said to old Brewster, 'if I have to swim for it.'

Brewster said weakly, 'I advise against this, Will. I realize you're a strong young man, but don't overlook the fact that you've been without rest for many hours and that water out there is very strong.' He made a little futile gesture. 'We could telephone around you know; could perhaps follow Sloat's progress that way. Surely there will be people see him go by. That way we could pinpoint the exact point where he stalls, if that happens.'

While Brewster was speaking Will lay a hand upon the door-knob. He wasn't listening. Neither was Pat. They were looking at one another.

'I'll be back,' he told her. 'The chances are Sloat'll get through all right on the tractor. You be prepared.'

She nodded and clasped both hands across her flat stomach. 'Will...? I'm sorry for the things that've been said tonight.'

He smiled gently. 'I'm not. At least it's out in the open.'

She moved quickly, stood on her tiptoes and kissed him squarely on the mouth. It startled them all. Her father blinked in the weak light. Gordon Johnson's mouth dropped open. She stepped back without dropping her eyes.

'Good luck, Will. We'll be waiting. Take care, won't you?'

He opened the door, stepped through, closed the door after himself and left Pat with the two elderly men standing in soggy silence. She didn't quite succeed in repressing a slight shudder, then turned and said, 'The fire needs building up,' and keeping her back to them went into the

112

parlour to toss on another log.

Johnson and old Brewster looked at one another, then shuffled into the parlour also.

The sound of rainfall was all around. Pat went upstairs to see how Catherine was getting on while her father and Gordon Johnson sat in chairs close to the fireplace.

'I've never seen the like of it,' mumbled Johnson. 'I think it's worse than the other storm.'

Brewster nodded without commenting. He was sombrely watching fresh flames leap and gyrate. The heat was good, of course, but there was a steadily increasing chill inside the house now; a kind of soggy gloominess that permeated everything but which particularly affected old bones and sinews. He leaned with both hands extended palms forward to the heat.

Gordon Johnson went out to telephone his residence. When he returned he told Brewster the Royal Engineers were in the southern sector of the village and had set up some kind of portable pump which, because of the lack of electrical power, they were using in conjunction with their lorry engines in some way. He also said his housekeeper had told him the radio was saying the storm was moving off, away from Harlham.

Of course that was comforting intelligence but sitting there listening to the raging torrents outside it was difficult to believe this was the truth.

Pat returned. Johnson told her what he'd heard. She went at once to get the small wireless from the kitchen and return it to the parlour. Fortunately it was one of those Japanese sets which worked either on transistors or electric current. She put it on the transistors and turned up the volume. There were three stations playing music and one giving the latest reports on the storm. They sat close to the fireplace listening to this latter station.

What Gordon Johnson had said was repeated. The storm centre had passed Harlham but, the announcer said, the rain would probably continue throughout most of the day, diminishing, he thought, perhaps in the middle of the afternoon until, by nightfall, it would have fallen off to a drizzle. He predicted neither wind nor rain for the following day.

She left the radio with Mr Johnson and

her father, went out to the little hall and telephoned round to see if anyone had seen Will Forman or had any news of Jeremy Sloat on his tractor.

No one had for the obvious reason that no one knew yet there was any drama outside their own four walls. The girl on the switchboard, however, promised to keep calling until everyone on the outskirts of the village had been alerted. She said she'd call Pat back the moment she had anything to report.

Paul Brewster got a shawl and offered it to Johnson, who declined it, so old Brewster put it about his own thin shoulders. It wasn't actually chilly but there was that dankness in the air not even a fireplace could quite dispel.

Also, through the shutters came the grey, watery brightness of dawn. Pat went over to open the shutters. At once the room was filled with that eerie, steely light.

As she returned to the fireplace Johnson asked her about the girl upstairs and her child. They were doing well, Pat said. Now that the wind had died Catherine would be able to sleep. She looked into the elderly faces. They weren't thinking of Catherine Everett, they were only using her as a means for getting their minds off Will.

The new day was worse than the darkness had been. There was a raging torrent in the road outside with an ominous hiss of water everywhere. She went to the window and stood looking out. Every house looked shiny and dark and strangely other-worldly.

She considered the force of the water, gazed at the fish-belly skies where rain came from in a monotonous, steady gush, and tried to imagine what it would be like at the lower end of the village where Sloat would be forcing his way against a river on his tractor and where Will would be, at least for the time being, moving with the force of the water.

How would he ever fight his way back against the current carrying an injured child?

She shuddered from the damp chilliness and caught hold of her lower lip with her teeth. He had been right and she'd been blind—there *were* different kinds of men. Perhaps, as he'd said, they all functioned more or less similarly because of chemistry, but there were degrees of decency, control,

116

manliness which varied greatly.

She turned. Her father was gazing solemnly over at her. He didn't speak and neither did she.

CHAPTER ELEVEN

The telephone operator called to say she'd had no word about either Jeremy Sloat or Will Forman. But—as though it would interest Pat—she said the Engineers had cleared two underground drains and were siphoning off a good deal of water in that way.

From the window in front of the house it didn't look as though much water was being siphoned off; that river out there was still two feet deep and raging.

She went upstairs to see how Catherine was doing. It required more effort up there to speak and be heard. The rainfall was a steady dirge over the rooftop.

Catherine asked about Will. Pat had told her earlier he'd gone out to meet Jeremy Sloat. She had no answer for the girl; no one had seen either Will or Sloat.

'Be a shame,' murmured young Catherine. 'Him being such a fine man and all.'

Pat stiffened. 'He's all right, I'm sure.'

'Are you? How long's he been gone an' why isn't he back by now?'

'Well, it would be very slow going you know. Moreover, I've no very clear idea just where they'll meet. It might be another half hour at the very least before he'd return.'

Catherine didn't argue the point but her expression remained melancholy.

Pat went to look at the little boy. He was sleeping as though there was no tumult directly overhead. Catherine said, 'He's going to be all right. It's his father's got me worried half to death.'

Pat changed the baby and changed the subject by saying, 'It's always seemed to me little boys wet a lot.'

Catherine raised her head to gaze at her son. She smiled with girlish, soft full lips. 'He can do as he likes mostly. Of course his father'll have to lay down the law now and again....' She raised eyes as blue as cornflowers to Pat. 'I wonder if he'll do it. He's not a very domineering man.'

Pat smiled. 'Then it'll be up to you, won't it?'

Catherine dropped her eyes to the baby again. 'No. Not I. Look at him. Could you ever spank him?'

It was a very handsome boy-baby. Looking at him now a person would have had to have been heartless to even think of spanking him, but Pat knew something little Catherine hadn't yet discovered: The most beautiful child on earth can, over the years, wear thin any parent's affection now and again.

'Can I get you something to eat, Catherine? Perhaps more tea?'

The cornflower-blue eyes lifted again. 'I'm not hungry. Just tired. Just weak as a kitten. But I want you to know we'll never be able to repay you. If it hadn't been for Mr Forman I'd probably have drowned out there. And him delivering the baby and all. I owe you folks so terribly much.'

Pat leaned, lifted away a lock of Catherine's hair, placed it gently to one side and said, 'Suppose it'd been me, and you'd been in my shoes...?'

'I'd probably have fainted dead away.'

They laughed together, then Pat went to the door. 'Sleep if you can, Catherine. Rest in any case; and if you want me rap on the floor.'

Out on the little gloomy landing she felt the chill sharply. Overhead the rainfall made a steady low roar. She went into her father's rumpled room where Gordon Johnson had been laid up, crossed to a window and considered the road first, then all the shimmering rooftops.

Oddly, Harlham was exactly as she remembered it. There was the water, of course, and there were signs of damage but otherwise nothing seemed changed.

She had the odd sensation of having just returned to the village after being absent for a long time, for many months or years.

She reflected on the elasticity of Time. One day seemed very short, another day seemed extraordinarily prolonged. Last night had seemed never to end. She was sure she'd never be a girl again; that in the lifetime she'd lived through thus far she'd aged greatly.

Her father calling from downstairs took her back to the little landing and swiftly downward. He and Gordon Johnson were standing there awaiting her, looking excited.

'The girl on the telephone just said someone on the outskirts saw two men with a big bundle driving very slowly up into town on a blue tractor. The men were drenched and the bundle they were carrying must be Jeremy's child.'

She made some rapid calculations. Harlham wasn't much of a town. Even granting Sloat's tractor was coming in low gear it still should arrive at the house within half an hour. Perhaps slightly more than half an hour but not much more.

'A bed,' she said, turned and ran back upstairs to her father's room. They'd need a bed for the injured child. She worked swiftly with sure, capable movements. Her heart pounded for some reason she didn't pause to analyse, and even if she had it might have told her she was simply reacting properly to an emergency—to the advent of the injured child—but that wasn't what had caused the tremendous feeling of relief.

He was safe.

When she returned to the lower floor her father and Gordon Johnson were in the parlour peering out of windows. They were fretfully saying there should be some sight of the tractor by now. She joined them, but when the anxiety got worse, she forced herself to go to put another log on the fire and stand for a moment with her back to the blaze.

She ached in a dozen different places. Her head didn't bother her, her wits were clear but she was physically exhausted. Just surviving the storm had taken a lot out of her—out of all of them. She thought of *him,* marvelling at his powerful endurance. She could recall nearly every sentence he'd said; could even recall the bitterness in his voice.

She felt her own emotions rising to meet his wishes which made her blush slightly. She knew what he was—a full man in every way that being a full man had significance. But there was more to him, much more, and it was this other quotient that kept her standing there feeling her soul reaching to him.

It was difficult to distinguish, to set each feeling she had apart from the confusion of all the other feelings, yet in sum total she recognized what it was that made her blush—she wanted him.

'They're coming!'

She came back to earth with a jolt. Her father was gesturing to her from the window. He was speaking loudly, too.

'By the Lord Harry's ghost they've made it!'

122

She hastened to the hall without bothering to peer out of the door. The parlour was warm and if the light coming inside was corpse-grey at least it was better than the terrifying total darkness of the night before.

She opened the door, tasted rain and moved aside as Will barged in carrying a bundle that smelt powerfully of animals—cattle and horses.

Will was drenched. So was Jeremy Sloat who entered immediately behind him with an ashen face and shock-dulled eyes. She took Will through to the parlour where he put the bundle upon a couch. The child inside was dry, thanks to the waterproof-canvas he'd been wrapped in. He had a pale look, his lips were blue and slack, while his eyes moved sluggishly as though he only half understood.

'Fracture,' Will murmured in her ear as he stepped back to make room. 'Jeremy,' he said to Sloat, 'come with me. We'll put these wet things in the kitchen.'

Sloat obeyed mechanically although his tortured eyes lingered on the slack little bundle where Pat was kneeling.

She hadn't time at that moment to be grateful to Will for taking the child's father into the kitchen, but later on she recalled this and thanked him. With Gordon Johnson and her father peering downward, she made her examination by grey dawnlight. The child wasn't more than ten or eleven years of age. He showed promise of having the same stocky, thick build his father also had.

Whatever it was that had struck him down left a dent in the skull. She probed very delicately to ascertain the extent of injury then went to the telephone and put in a call to the next village for the doctor there. She got through, which was a miracle in itself, but the woman who took the call said the doctor was out on an emergency.

Pat left word what had happened; she wanted the doctor to come to Harlham as soon as he possibly could. The woman, sounding distraught, said that would be quite impossible; not only were the roads impassable, but the doctor had his hands full in his own village.

Pat hung up and stood like stone. She was still standing like that when Will and Jeremy Sloat came back from the kitchen. Sloat only glanced at her then hastened past her to be with his son. Will, though, catching sight of her face, halted and turned back.

She looked up at him. 'The doctor isn't at home and his wife says he can't possibly get to Harlham.'

She was leaning on him, waiting for whatever he'd say, searching for help or guidance or both. He continued to regard her for a long while before he spoke. 'The boy must be taken to hospital; he'll probably need surgery.'

'I know.'

He scowled. 'I'd be afraid of trying to get to the next village with him on that tractor and no car could get through.'

'Will, that child is going to die.'

He said a swear word. 'Nonsense. That child'll pull through.'

'How? Just tell me how?'

He shook his head, still scowling at her. 'You've got some drugs, haven't you?'

'Drugs? Will, there's no drug in the world that can—'

'Keep him sedated,' he ordered harshly. 'Keep him from moving, from threshing about. You've got opiates haven't you?'

'Yes, of course but that will only be a temporary aid.'

'Dammit, I know that, Pat. Just do as

I say!' He spun and headed straight back for the kitchen. She ran after him. He'd made some kind of decision. She had to know what it was.

He was struggling back into the sodden coat and cap when she burst into the kitchen and halted. 'You're not going out again?'

'Will staying here be any help?' he demanded.

'Where will you go? What possible good can you do?'

'Get the child to a doctor. That's what's got to be done, isn't it?'

She moved up in front as though to block his way. 'You can't. You said yourself hauling him about on that tractor—'

'I'm not going to haul him anywhere.' He was going to say more but he didn't. He reached, caught her by the shoulders and gave her a hard little shake. 'Get hold of yourself, Pat. He'll pull through. Just trust me and pray.'

She felt the bite of his fingers, felt the power of his will. 'I'll trust you,' she told him, 'and I'll pray, but it's going to take more than that, Will.'

'Is it?' he said harshly, and wrenched her to him. The soggy coat was cold.

She threw up both hands, palms against his chest. 'You're damned right it's going to take more than trust,' he said. 'It's going to take *faith.*' He lifted her face, brought his mouth down, hard, and kissed her, then he roughly pushed her away and started past.

But this time she wasn't caught unprepared. As he swung past she lunged, caught his sleeve and yanked him back around.

'I have enough faith,' she said, and pulled him closer, stood on tiptoe and kissed him squarely on the mouth. He stood like a stone, his eyes jumping wide open. She reached and gave him a push. 'All right. You're going to fetch the doctor on the tractor. Go. Hurry!'

He moved slowly, then he turned back at the door and smiled at her. 'By God you're all the woman my instincts told me you were, Pat.'

'Go!'

'Sure. But I didn't have in mind bringing back the doctor.'

He left. She stood in the middle of the kitchen trying to fathom what he'd said. If he didn't have in mind bringing back the doctor what *did* he have in mind?

Her father came into the kitchen looking pale. 'Will just went out the front door,' he said. 'Where is he going, Pat?'

'I don't know, Father.'

'You don't know?'

'No. But I have faith. He'll think of something. Trust him.'

Old Brewster looked hard at his daughter. He hadn't seen that look of life in her eyes for six years.

CHAPTER TWELVE

She had to answer questions when she returned to the parlour. Jeremy Sloat wanted to know what she could do for his young son. He also wanted to know what the child's chances were.

It was necessary to be evasive, which she didn't like at all. It was also necessary to keep the child relaxed so she gave him the first mild injection, then, to turn his father's mind from the immediate present, asked how the injury had been incurred.

Sloat, who'd often enough demonstrated a rough wit and garrulousness at the Coach and Four, was singularly troubled now. The children, he said with many starts and stops, had been in the loft of their old farmhouse listening to the storm. They would go up there now and again to gauge the intensity of wind and water on the roof. There were some old bits of cured oak up there left over from the Lord-knew-when. As the children moved about one of them had dislodged one of those old oak baulks, the thing had dropped and struck Jeremy's little son squarely on his head.

Jeremy excused himself briefly now that Pat was there and left the room. Gordon Johnson took his opportunity to insist on knowing exactly what the child's chances were. She didn't tell him but when her father also asked she gently shook her head from side to side. 'It will take a miracle,' she murmured.

There were darkening circles under the child's eyes. He'd seemed gently relaxed even before she'd made sure of it. There didn't seem much possibility he'd regain total consciousness again until the pressure was relieved, but she couldn't take the chance; he had to be kept motionless and quiet.

Jeremy returned to say he'd telephone

his wife to reassure her. She still had the other two Sloat children with her at home.

Pat diverted him a little by asking about the storm. He'd lost the roof from an outbuilding and there'd been some damage otherwise around the farm. Nothing he couldn't repair in good time, but on his ride to the village he'd noticed other damage. Esau Gibbon's place for example, had also lost a roof from an outbuilding, and rain had cut bad gashes in Gibbon's hillsides.

Pat suggested that her father offer Mr Sloat some thing to take the bone-chilling dampness out of him, which her father at once did, taking Sloat into the kitchen with him.

Left alone with Gordon Johnson, Pat rose from the chair beside her latest patient and said she was going to look in on Catherine upstairs. She wanted Mr Johnson to mind the unconscious lad.

He spluttered but in the end agreed, took her vacated chair and admonished her to hasten back, saying that if the child moved he'd not know what to do, but even had he known, with only one arm functioning wouldn't be able to do it.

She hastened. Cathering was nursing her newborn son. She smiled at Pat, saying she'd been thinking, and that she was more fortunate than she'd originally thought, because in the Brewster home she was permitted to keep her baby with her while in a hospital they'd have been parted at birth.

There was no reason for Pat to linger, both Catherine and her infant son were coming along famously. She made several changes, asked if Catherine were hungry yet, then went to the window to pull the curtains fully open, and saw for the first time that the rain was diminishing.

She should have known from the lessening gusts overhead but hadn't heeded that until now. She tried to see up or down the road. The blue tractor was gone but that came as no surprise at all.

It was possible finally to make out smoke rising from several chimneys. Rain might shatter it before the smoke rose very high, but at least, unlike that wild wind of the night before, the rain couldn't sweep it away almost as soon as it'd left the smoke-stacks.

She turned. Catherine was watching her from the bed, the cornflower-blue eyes wiser than the piquant face they belonged to.

'He'll get there, Miss Brewster.'

Pat was surprised. She hadn't mentioned that Will had left again—or had she. With heavy limbs she moved back to the bed. 'Of course he will. I don't know how we'd have managed tonight without him.'

Catherine agreed. 'He's wonderful. So rugged and strong and...well, handsome too, don't you think, Miss Brewster?'

Pat smiled, bent to adjust the coverlets and ran a gentle finger over the head of Catherine's son. 'Has your husband got black hair too?' she asked.

Catherine looked downward with an expression of perplexity, forgetting entirely about Will Forman as she answered. 'No; neither have I, neither have our parents. I'm worried about it on our son. Shouldn't I be, Miss Brewster?'

Pat said it would change colour, promised to return when she could, and returned to the downstairs parlour.

Jeremy and her father were evidently still in the kitchen but Gordon Johnson was enormously relieved when she came in.

He'd been watching the child, he said, and thought he'd seen the eyelids flutter as though the boy were coming round. He wasn't regaining consciousness, Pat explained; the moving eyelids were typical of someone in his predicament.

Johnson rose to give her the chair and said, 'What possible good can Forman do running over half the countryside searching for a surgeon on that blue tractor? I've a notion half the roads are washed out anyway.'

She didn't answer because she was taking the Sloat child's pulse. It was low but not distressingly so. Of course, if the boy weren't helped soon, it wouldn't only be his pulse which would sink.

Her father and Jeremy came out of the kitchen, crossed through both the dining-room and entrance hall, then noiselessly approached the couch where young Sloat still lay unmoving. Jeremy would have spoken but Pat held up her hand silencing him. She hadn't done that because the child needed silence—he couldn't hear what they were saying in any event. She did it to forestall answering a lot of questions for which she actually had no real answers.

The three men went across to the roadway window and stood in gloomy silence looking out. Johnson said it seemed to him the rain was lessening somewhat. Pat's father concurred and also pointed out that unless his eyes deceived him, the floodwaters in the roadway were receding.

Perhaps they were receding, but if they were it was such a slow and minute recession the three men had to watch closely, selecting levels to watch, to be sure this was so.

It all helped. Pat sat gazing tiredly into the fireplace thankful for every moment that passed when she didn't have to reassure Jeremy. She just wasn't up to giving that much of herself any more. There was so little strength left in her.

She worried too, which was natural, and although she tried to prevent it, her thoughts kept turning to that last, brief and explosive meeting between herself and Will Forman.

She could faintly smile in recollecting the look of utter astonishment on his face when she'd wrenched him around then had planted that hard kiss squarely upon his lips.

Of course, a thing like that thrust their acquaintanceship upon a fresh level. It wouldn't be possible to return to the earlier levels of Mr and Miss. Or to their furious little angry exchanges. That voluntary kiss on her part had done away in one second with all the formalities.

She wondered, when he returned, what their attitude would be towards one another. She also thought of what little Catherine Everett had said, and while she'd changed the subject upstairs, now, alone with her private thoughts by the fireplace, she agreed. He *was* handsome.

Education prompted her to consider the question of propinquity; they'd been held together in a confining, tense atmosphere since the day before. She'd seen him use his strength several times. He'd given of himself without thought of the consequences. He'd been the youngest, strongest, most eligible man around her for what seemed now to have been ten years of terror telescoped into one horrifying night.

Of course she'd been drawn to him. That was a physical and very natural thing. If there'd been four or five other young, strong men around, would she have come to feel for him as she now privately admitted she felt?

The answer came gently. Yes, she'd feel

the same because he'd still have done all those things; he'd still have stood out above any other men for the elementary reason that where most men would have hesitated, would have advanced dozens of excuses for *not* facing the full fury of the storm, he'd have gone out each time.

She sighed, her body loosening in the chair, her spirit conserving its own strength for whatever lay ahead. If it hadn't been for the Sloat child she'd have gone upstairs to lie down for an hour or two. In fact, if it hadn't been for the pitiful little limp, grey-faced child at her side, she'd have given a great sigh of relief, for Catherine Everett was doing well, Gordon Johnson's arm was properly set and giving its owner no pain, and the storm was dying, which meant the battle was nearly over. Not won, of course; as long as the Sloat child lay there, defeat lurked for them all despite their sacrifices, but otherwise it would have been so easy just to go upstairs to bed, blot out everything that had happened by simply lying down and closing her eyes.

She didn't hear nor sense the approach

of her father until he thrust a cup of something warm into her hand. 'Toddy,' he said. 'Not a substitute for genuine energy but an excellent catalyst.'

She sipped. The toddy was made of something with ginger in it, and rum. It actually tasted rather good. She smiled her thanks and sipped.

Jeremy Sloat came over also with a cup of the same mixture. He considered his limp child, looked at Pat and seemed to understand how tired she was. He said, softly and gruffly, 'When a man is young nothing touches him. He has his dreams, his work, his strength and his will. But time is against him although he doesn't realize it. Then things don't come off quite as he'd planned. He begins to realize a lot of things he hadn't any time to look at before. What it all sums up to, Miss Patience, is the learnin' of patience. Like your name. I got to be patient now, although I don't know why, and I've lived this long: I know what I got to do.'

She listened, then looked up at the weathered, tough face with its sunken, stricken eyes. 'Will said just before he left that we must have faith, Mr Sloat.'

'Ay. I'll have it for as long as a man can, Miss Brewster, but I don't suppose you'll ever know what it does to a father's insides, standing like I've got to do now, looking at my son.'

Her father suggested they drink down their toddies so that he could refill the cups but neither of them heeded him. The child was there to prevent either Pat or Jeremy from thinking of anything else.

She told Sloat of Catherine Everett upstairs. He nodded as though he already knew, which he probably did since he'd been in the kitchen for some while with her father.

She told him about Joan Eaton's stomach upset too, but that seemed a very long while ago as she sat recalling it now.

They spoke all around the topic uppermost in all their minds. Gordon Johnson, still over by the front window, interrupted after a bit with a loud snort and a whinnying curse.

'He's done it again, damned if he hasn't!'

Pat leapt up. The two older men also whirled to rush forward. Johnson was beside himself fidgeting and gesturing.

Outside, coming slowly but surely up the road splashing through water with its big wheels was a rain-shiny tan lorry with a covered top and the insignia of the Royal Engineers on it. Rain ran in rivulets off the bonnet, down the sides of the huge vehicle, and although the windscreen wipers were furiously whipping to and fro rain fell too strongly for any of the breathless watchers to be able to determine who was in the cab.

The great vehicle slowed, feeling its way, veered towards the kerb outside the Brewster house, and Pat heard Jeremy Sloat whisper: 'I thank the Lord.'

She saw Will spring down on the far side, a stocky, shorter man climb out on the kerb side. He was dressed in a shiny waterproof and beat his hands together while waiting for Will to come round to him. He shouted something which Will probably didn't hear as he led the way towards the front door.

All four people by the window turned as one and hastened to the door. The lorry sat in water almost to the hubs puffing out wispy little white puffs of smoke while it waited.

CHAPTER THIRTEEN

Sergeant Carmody's first name was Winston, and after he'd shed his waterproof, had shaken hands all round, his merry blue eyes twinkled as he said his father had been a great admirer 'Of the old gentleman.' He didn't elaborate. There'd not been too many prominent Winstons in British history.

While he was led into the parlour by Pat's father and Jeremy, Gordon Johnson lingered in the entry to splutter out some highly complimentary comments to Will, who looked now, in wet daylight, as though he hadn't shaved for several days instead of just one night and day.

Pat put her hand on Will's arm. Johnson saw this, seemed suddenly to recall something, turned and hastened into the parlour to join the others. Pat said, 'How did you ever do it?'

Will dripped water as he said, 'All this traffic is going to thoroughly wet the carpets.'

She closed strong fingers down upon his forearm holding him motionless. 'I asked a question, Will Forman.'

He lifted tired eyes that almost smiled at her. 'Well, *how* I did it isn't really so important. *Why* I did it ought to be obvious. Some beautiful girl kissed me just before I left, and I swear to you it was better than a four-course meal, ten hours rest, and a glass of scotch. I was so re-energized I simply—'

She removed her hand from his arm. He was smiling at her, almost laughing at her in fact. She smiled back with colour mounting up under both cheeks.

'I'd no idea I had such power,' she murmured.

'I did. I knew it from the first day I saw you.'

'Will...you've distinguished yourself to-night. Joking aside.'

He stopped smiling but his gaze lingered, still soft towards her. 'We haven't run the race yet, old girl. The soldiers were about where I expected to find them. It didn't take much persuading to get them to loan us a driver and one of their lorries. But they happen to have a wireless in one of their vehicles... They were informed about an hour ago that the main roadway is washed out in two places.'

She didn't falter. 'But there are other roads. Surely the sergeant can navigate them.'

'If they're not washed out too, love. And there's one more thing. The child can be made perfectly dry and comfortable in the lorry. It's properly covered. But everyone can't go.'

'Why not?'

Will looked upwards. 'What about Catherine Everett?'

Pat thought a moment. 'My father and Mr Johnson can stay here. Neither of them would be much help on the road anyway.'

He looked straight at her. Evidently he'd been of the opinion she'd remain with Catherine and send her father on with the lorry. He nodded. Her plan was good enough providing the Everett girl wasn't likely to need any professional help.

He made some such comment. She said the main thing Catherine needed now, and would continue to need for several days, was quiet, plenty of rest, nourishing food and her infant son beside her. Then she said, 'You didn't want me to come along on the lorry?'

'Want you? There's no place I ever expect to go I wouldn't want you to come too. But I wasn't thinking of what *I* want.'

She put her head slightly to one side. 'Maybe you should think like that, Will.'

He stood sombrely studying her. 'Pat, don't play games with me.'

She smiled into his eyes feeling the thrill of his closeness and what they were saying to one another without using any of the clichés or the actual words. This was the first time they could do that as mates; if the feeling continued though, they'd be able to do it many times afterwards.

'We'd better get the patient into the lorry,' she said, and laid her fingers lightly upon his arm again. 'I'm not playing games with you, Will.'

He followed her into the parlour where the others were. Sergeant Carmody's blue eyes lifted, raked once up and down Pat, then widened with strong appreciation. Evidently youthful Sergeat Carmody was a man who admired handsome women. He'd have been a very rare soldier indeed if he hadn't admired them.

143

He said, looking at Pat but apparently addressing Will, 'You've about hit it on the head, mate. The lad's bad off. But I think, if we take all this canvas and whatnot along, we can make him a good enough pallet in the back.' He smiled round at them all. He was, evidently, a tough, resourceful, cheery man, one of those rugged, stocky individuals to whom adversity was a challenge, never a discouragement.

'Miss, if you'll ride in the back with Mr Forman to see the lad doesn't bounce round, these other gentlemen can ride up front with me. Plenty of—'

'They'll be staying,' she said. Her father and Gordon Johnson looked up quickly. Sergeant Carmody said, 'Not the lad's father, Miss. He'll be coming along won't he?'

'He will, yes, but the others won't.' When Gordon might have protested Pat said, 'I can't very well be in two places at once. Someone has to stay and watch over Catherine and the baby.'

Johnson's puffed out cheeks deflated. Old Brewster's expression altered softly. He nodded. Not pleased but understanding.

Sergeant Carmody motioned. 'Lend a

hand,' he ordered. 'Cover his face until we're inside the lorry. Mind that canvas now; I should imagine keeping him dry'll be important.'

He barked at them but he also was correct in everything he told them to do. 'Keep the canvas taut now; no sagging in the middle. That's it. Steady on now. Miss; the front door please....'

She barely had time to snatch up her coat and hat after opening the door for them. She ran out into the cold water without her wellingtons. She didn't even remember them until both shoes filled with water that was cold enough to make her gasp.

The bed of the lorry seemed impossibly high but the men managed. Will extended a hand to her, pulled her up easily, then straightened up as Carmody and the others raised the burden to him. Jeremy sprang up to assist.

The sound of rain on the lorry's top was like a hundred distant drums because the inside of the vehicle was empty except for fold-down narrow wooden benches on each side.

Carmody suggested putting the lad on the floor of the lorry. 'The benches'll be too narrow; he'd topple off if we hit any rough stretches...I've reason to believe we'll hit.'

Gordon hadn't climbed up. No one had offered him a hand and he couldn't get up alone using only one arm. Rain darkened his suit almost at once. Pat's father too, after seeing the lad made comfortable, climbed out. They stood in the downpour looking forlorn.

Carmody ran round, climbed up and tried to start the engine a time or two, then eased the huge transport into low gear and eased out his clutch. To the people inside the sound of displaced water sounded ominous. Behind them, hands held high, Paul Brewster and Gordon Johnson stood knee-deep in the flooded roadway, then turned and struggled back to the kerb and beyond, to the dryness and warmth of the house.

Pat sat cross-legged on one side of the bundled child. Jeremy sat on the other side. They concentrated on cushioning the boy from any jolts or lurches.

Will sat nearer the back and watched the village move away on either side of them. Sergeant Carmody didn't know the vicinity but he had an excellent map with him on the front seat. He and Will had already discussed the routes, direct and alternate. Will had suggested the secondary road they eventually got upon after he'd been informed the main road had been washed out. He stood back there now, one hand gripping a strap-hanger, assessing the damage and watching their course to be certain Sergeant Carmody didn't turn off on a wrong road.

There appeared to be more damage at the upper end of Harlham where the homes and shops weren't built together as continuous blocks. He pointed out a roofless cottage and farther along, the flattened corrugated iron roof of a barn.

They passed two cars heeled over into a ditch looking somewhat like sunken ships. Trees had been uprooted and one had crashed down across a stone wall sending pieces of flat slag in all directions.

The countryside too, seemed drowned. More so in fact than the village. Water stood everywhere, making veritable lakes out of fields. Fortunately, after a mile or two, there were markers to show where the road was. Hedges helped too, for otherwise it would have been impossible in some places to know where a field ended and the roadway began.

Sergeant Carmody drove carefully; he'd have had no alternative even if he hadn't had the critically injured passenger for he was driving against a strong current every yard of the way.

Will went back, after a while, and knelt beside Pat. She smiled, indicating that so far the lad was doing quite well. Jeremy looked up too. He didn't smile but he inclined his head either in agreement with Pat or in approval of the way Sergeant Carmody was carrying on.

It wasn't cold inside the huge vehicle even though the rear of the thing was open and exposed. It wasn't really very cold out anyway. There was no sunshine but it was daylight and the day was far enough advanced to offer some warmth. Even the rainwater, except where it was being confined by stone or metal, seemed warmer.

Will explained that he'd chosen this road they were travelling. He gave his valid reasons. Pat and Jeremy nodded; they seemed less interested in the route than in the lad they were caring for, which was natural enough.

Will went forward until he could sit with

his back to the metal rear of the cab. There, slumping into his soggy clothing, he closed his eyes. The others didn't know he was asleep until Jeremy happened to glance back. He said something and Pat also turned. Her comment was louder.

'He's deserved it. He's been dead on his feet since midnight.'

'He's a good man,' affirmed Jeremy, gazing at the whiskery, grey face back there in the gloom. 'He's been a hard one t'know, I'll tell you that for a fact. Me'n the missus often said Mr Forman didn't seem to quite fit around Harlham. he's been everywhere, done so many things... This is a country place, Miss Brewster. Simple ways and simple folk. But I'll tell you—I thank the Lord he was amongst us last night and today.'

She said nothing although Sloat's rough words warmed her immensely. She gently tucked an old none-too-clean blanket under the unconscious child's chin and made certain he was covered elsewhere as well.

'Strong he is,' said Sloat, still gazing back where Will slumped, head lolling forward. 'Strong and tough as an old boot. Seems odd though, him being a chemist. His type's usually the police, or a professional soldier, something rugged if you know what I mean.'

She knew but she didn't concur. The world was full of quiet men of great strength, chemists and other things equally tame perhaps, but let an emergency arise....

She said, 'Mr Sloat, we never really know people until there is a disaster, do we?'

'No'm, don't suppose we do.'

The lorry lurched, slowed to a crawl and gradually righted itself as it waddled up out of the hole in the roadway. Carmody's cheery, tough voice sang out. 'Sorry; didn't have an inkling about that 'un. Usually they got little whirlpools in the water above 'em. That 'un didn't. I'll watch closer.'

The unconscious youth had sagged slightly but otherwise, wrapped as he was, he hardly moved as the lorry floundered.

His father looked up, white in the face. 'I thought we'd stopped.'

Pat had for a second entertained the same fear—and dread. If anything stopped them now, miles from Harlham miles from their destination as well, in an impassably drowned countryside, there would have been no way under the sun to help the Sloat child.

She was tense for a mile or two afterwards, praying against her fear that nothing would appear to make them stop.

The rain kept up its drum-roll on the top and sides of the big lorry. It made conversation difficult so she and Jeremy fell silent. There was nothing they could do now but wait, protect the child, and hope as hard as they could this would all end right.

She looked back after another hour and saw that Will had slid down; that he was lying with his head cushioned on one arm, dead asleep. She felt proud of him, and tender towards him. Whether he liked the term or not he definitely *had* been heroic!

CHAPTER FOURTEEN

The lorry stopped. Pat felt her stomach harden into a knot. She and Jeremy exchanged a look of agony. They were mid-way or thereabouts between the village they'd left and the village which was their destination. All around was the drowned, grey and battered countryside.

Sergeant Carmody's head and shoulders appeared over the tailgate. He looked at them, looked elsewhere, finally spotted Will and called sharply to him. Will didn't respond until Pat leaned back and shook him gently.

He sat up, saw Carmody, looked round, seemed to realize finally they were no longer moving, and shoved heavily up to his feet.

'What is it?' he called to Carmody. 'Flooded out?'

Carmody shook his head, pursed his lips then called back through the rainfall. 'There's a bridge...come have a look with me.'

Pat suddenly recalled the bridge. Evidently so did Jeremy because he started to rise stiffly to his feet. He didn't say anything to Pat. He didn't have to. As Will dropped down off the rear of the lorry Jeremy followed after him.

She closed her eyes the better to visualize that bridge. She'd come over this road many times but the entire countryside looked so different now she'd quite forgotten the bridge. Now, trying hard to recall it, all she came up with was a general picture. She'd never had occasion to pay close attention to the thing anyway.

There was a deep chasm and at the bottom of it, perhaps thirty feet down, a small stream ran across from right to left underneath the road. The bridge was stone and old. She remembered the lichen upon it, and some nearly obliterated stone symbols of some kind. The bridge was perhaps a hundred years old or more and she was worried whether the flooding had undermined it.

That of course was also what the engineering sergeant, Will Forman and Jeremy Sloat also anxiously wished to ascertain. If they couldn't cross they'd have to go back many miles and try another road. The delay could be fatal. Already Jeremy's child had been in a coma without proper care as long as he should have been.

Pat felt the cold chill of impending disaster for all of them. She struggled against it, bent to see that her little patient was secure and when she raised her head Will was gazing at her over the tailgate. He wasn't smiling. Evidently Sergeant Carmody and Jeremy were still out in front of the lorry, perhaps on the bridge.

Will climbed in, came back and knelt. She had no difficulty in guessing his thoughts, they were stamped on his features.

'It's impossible to tell,' he said, referring to the bridge, 'whether it's seriously undermined or not. There's too much water out there, and going out on to the thing and springing up and down doesn't help much. None of us has anywhere near the weight of the lorry.'

She had a premonition. Will was going to take the lorry across. She said, 'Is there any other way?'

He nodded. 'Several other ways in fact, Pat, but each one will require going back several miles, then branching off, and there is no guarantee the other roads won't also be washed out.'

'So,' she said, 'you're going to drive across.'

He considered her a moment before answering. 'It's a chance we have to take. The others will help you out with the boy.'

'You're going to take it across alone, Will?' She felt the knot in her stomach tighten still more.

'No, Sergeant Carmody will go too.'

'And if,' she said, 'the bridge collapses, then what? This child will be out here on the wet ground without a single hope left. He'll die long before anyone comes along, Will.'

He kept watching her face as he inclined his head at her again. He'd evidently already considered that prospect. 'What do you want to do?' he asked quietly, so quietly in fact his words were nearly lost in the down-pour. 'If we turn round and go back there's an excellent chance that by now we can't even reach Harlham. If we take one of the other roads, it might also be washed out. If we cross over and make it, the boy will live. If we fall through he won't. Pat, the chances are three-to-one against Jeremy's child.'

'Will, you can be killed!'

'I doubt that. Even if we fall through, the distance is only thirty or so feet with water to cushion the shock. Even granting the current is swift and swollen, Carmody thinks it's a good gamble.'

'There's no such thing as a *good* gamble. Will.'

He waited a moment, then reached forth, dropped a hand to her shoulder and said, 'Don't panic, Pat. We've got to take the chance. It's the only *real* chance the child has. Going back will almost surely doom him and you know it.'

'But I don't want you to be—'

'Faith, love, faith,' he crooned, and bent to lift her lips and kiss them. She would have reached to cling to him but he rocked back. There were tears of terror in her eyes. If he noticed that he gave no indication of it. His face was dark, wet and set in a tough, hard expression. 'Come along; I'll help you down, then Jeremy can help you with the child.'

Sergeant Carmody came round the back of the van, looked up, saw the tears and let his mouth droop in sympathy. Jeremy came along a moment later. They got his unconscious child out of the lorry. Carmody took hold of Pat's hand and gave it a little squeeze. 'He's right, you know, Miss; if we don't make it the lad's no worse off than if we turn about and try another road. It's bitter but it's true.' He released her and hastened forward through the pelting downpour to climb up into his lorry. Will had already gone round and mounted up from the opposite side.

Jeremy's lips were moving as the lorry

began inching ahead. He apparently was praying and praying hard. Pat felt the cooling rain upon her face. She reached, found Sloat's thick arm and held to it with both hands as she watched.

The lorry had dual wheels behind. Its overall appearance was cumbersome, very heavy and out of scale with its sodden surroundings. It resembled an immense bug of some kind with a shiny shell. The little puffs of smoke seemed to be evenly spaced as the vehicle lifted its blunt and ugly snout slightly, upon the approaches to the bridge. Pat wasn't aware of tightening her grip on Sloat's arm. He was holding his son cradled against his thick body and staring from squinted eyes.

The lorry got well up on to the bridge approach, settled slightly as it levelled off, then it was upon the bridge itself. Pat had trouble in breathing. She wanted to scream at Carmody and Will to hasten, to increase their speed and hurtle on across. They couldn't have heard her, but had they it was doubtful that they'd have obeyed.

The bridge was solid, they knew that from having walked across it and back again, but otherwise, it being under more than a foot of water, there was no way to be sure they would drop a wheel through a hole and be hung up there until the lorry's weight collapsed the timbers. In fact there was no way to be certain of anything.

Jeremy said, 'Now—whatever happens will be now!'

Carmody and Will were directly in the centre of the bridge. Pat and Jeremy could no longer even hear the throaty growl of the truck. They could see it distantly, as though it were some ghostly behemoth sluggishly waddling ahead, but there was no sound coming back through the roar of water.

The lorry rocked drunkenly and Pat stifled a scream. Jeremy's hold on his son tightened. They stood like stone carvings.

The lorry lurched ahead, slewing half around from the force of all that surging water. Carmody fought it forward again, gave it a bit more pedal and it waddled the last twenty feet, tilted its tailgate and moved with agonizing slowness down the far approach and on to the solid roadbend again.

Pat loosened her grip on Sloat's arm. She saw Will and Carmody spring down and come back towards them. She said, 'Let's cross over, Mr Sloat.' It was an unnecessary remark for Jeremy was already moving. Pat thought there were tears on his cheeks but that might only have been more rain. She knew she was crying. She also knew the rain would hide that for her too.

Carmody was beaming. Will didn't smile but as he reached for Jeremy's bundle he shouted above the roar of water. 'There has to be *some* good luck now and then.'

They got the child back into the lorry, climbed in themselves and were off again. Will shook like a dog getting rid of surplus water. Jeremy sat beside his son with streams running off him which he totally disregarded.

Pat wiped her face with a soggy handkerchief, removed her hat and shook out her hair, which was dry. She waited until Will had dropped to one knee beside her than beckoned as though she wished to whisper. When he bent close she kissed him. Jeremy saw that and looked startled, but only for a moment. He then leaned far over and pushed his extended hand out. 'I'll not be *that* grateful, Mr Forman, but I'd like to shake your hand.'

Will shook, smiled at Pat and sank down closer to her. Behind them the bridge was already lost to sight. They were moving through a grey mist which, except for the rain, would undoubtedly have been a thick fog.

'Something to be thankful for,' he said, pointing outside. 'Under the circumstances I'd prefer a little less water, but anything would be preferable to fog.'

They broke through the water with their wheels making wide waves to the rear, then the road climbed and for the first time they were out of water. Near the crest Pat said, 'I think we're going to make it. Will. I think my prayers have been answered.'

He nodded. The village which was their destination lay only another two miles beyond the crest of the low hill. He lay back, soaked to the skin, put the cap her father had lent him under his head, closed his eyes and was asleep in moments. When Jeremy looked over he nodded as though approving of this.

Pat made a few minor adjustments of the canvas around the child, put her cramped legs in a different position, speculated on how much difficulty they'd have in finding the doctor, then settled to watch the drowned countryside beyond the tailgate.

Sergeant Carmody halted again, but this

time he didn't waken Will he simply came round to ask Pat to come up in front and ride with him because he had no idea where to go once they got into the village. She obliged.

It was warm inside the cab. Too warm in fact and Carmody made some adjustment on his panel to take care of that. The seat wasn't soft but it was a vast improvement on the iron bed of the van section of their lorry.

'Quite a man,' said Carmody conversationally, 'your Mr Forman. He'd be terrific in uniform.'

She nodded agreement but said nothing. Carmody then said, 'About this doctor on ahead—you certain we'll find him?'

'We've *got* to find him, Sergeant.'

Carmody thought about that a moment then said, 'All right, Miss, we'll find him. After all, he can't get very far in all this, can he?'

That hadn't occurred to her but now, thinking about it, she felt great relief. Of course Carmody was right; the doctor wouldn't be very far away.

The village came out to them, sodden and glistening, with a faint aroma of woodsmoke in the grey daylight. She told

Carmody where to turn off the main road and which house belonged to the man they sought. As he eased the lorry in beside the kerb he reached to tap her shoulder and offer a big, wide grin.

'Royal Engineers always come through.'

They went round to the back where Will and Jeremy were already unloading their patient. Pat felt the scald of tears again but as before the rain disguised them. As Will and Jeremy started towards the house Will twisted his head to say, 'The rain's lifting, Pat. Look up.' When she obeyed he caught her easily and kissed her. Carmody was startled but this time Jeremy didn't see it.

A greying woman had the door open. She'd obviously seen them from inside the house. She stepped far back so that they could squeeze in, then she closed the door and looked in total astonishment at them. To Pat she said, 'You're not the ones as called from Harlham...?'

Pat nodded, unable for a moment to speak. Will cut in to ask if the doctor was at home. The woman nodded and motioned for them to follow her with the unconscious child. She looked at each of them very hard as though unable to believe they'd actually driven through the worst storm in local history all the way from Harlham.

Pat could scarcely believe it herself, but she was almost drugged by now with fatigue and went docilely along behind Will.

CHAPTER FIFTEEN

The medical practitioner was a rather short, grey, grizzled, confident man of perhaps sixty. When his wife made the introductions he took them into an examination room, had the child put upon a high, metal table and told them all to leave the room except Pat, whom he knew.

He was quiet, thorough, and candid. 'Quite a bump,' he eventually said, bending low. 'The lad must have a cranium of solid bone. Yeoman stock I'd suspect; they usually are thick-skulled...thick-headed too in my opinion.'

The waspish monotone ran on throughout the entire examination punctuated now and again with a question. How had they got here; whatever made them think they'd succeed without killing the lad jostling him about in a lorry; how much damage had the storm done back in Harlham.

Pat answered the questions and otherwise watched the examination. She was dreading the judgement she had feared most since she'd first seen Jeremy's child: He'd have to go up to one of the major hospitals in London.

The delay had gone on just about as long as they dared let it. She knew it and was certain, as he straightened back, the village doctor knew it. He turned, went to a cabinet, stood gazing through the glass at the glistening instruments, turned and fixed Pat with a hard, blue stare.

'You are aware of the need for prompt surgery,' he said to her. It wasn't a question; he wasn't asking her opinion, he was instead using her for a sounding-board for himself. He was actually arguing with himself.

'The facilities are available. Not the best of course, but then we're not in London, are we? The operation is not terribly difficult nor complicated. We'll need parental approval of course, and we'll need to get on with it too. I'm sure you are aware of the perils of additional delay.

'Well, Miss Brewster, it's a challenge all round. Please go with me to speak with the lad's father.'

Jeremy wasn't far off. He was loitering in fact just outside the examination room where the doctor's wife had brought something hot for Sloat, Will and the sergeant.

The doctor explained in crisp and vivid language what was required. He did not do any of it in the manner of a man seeking to win a popularity contest. In fact when Will asked how long the surgery would take and if the weakened boy was up to it, he answered:

'My dear Mr Forman, the lad is weak, yet physically he's in excellent condition. The longer we stand about out here making a lot of pointless conversation, the weaker he's going to get. I can promise nothing, yet I'm rather confident of the outcome. Mr Sloat, it's up to you. He's your child.'

Sloat nodded. 'Go ahead, Doctor.'

Pat wasn't surprised at Jeremy's decision. There was no other way. Whether the child lived or died under the knife, at least he had a chance to survive. Without the operation he had no chance at all.

She said, 'I'll go to scrub up, Doctor.'

'You,' he said, turning, 'will do nothing of the sort. You and your friends here will find rooms at the end of the corridor. They are warm, there are beds and blankets there. There is a bathroom mid-way along the hall. You people will get some rest.'

They stood looking at him. Pat started to protest. The doctor cut her off with an upraised hand. 'My wife was the best surgical nurse in the country when we were married. She's been with me through two-thirds of all my operations. She'll work with me this time as well.'

The doctor turned, re-entered the examination room and closed the door. For Pat it was a let-down. She looked at Will, at Jeremy Sloat and the sergeant feeling less rejected than just plain useless. She'd steeled herself for that final effort. Now it had been denied her.

Will moved up a chair for her. 'Gruff old bird,' he said soothingly, 'but I'm betting he'll bring it off. He may be right about this choice of nurse too, Pat. If his wife's that good...'

She considered her hands. They were wrinkled from water, the fingernails broken. Will looked round. Jeremy wasn't paying either of them the least attention. He was sitting hunched far over holding his cup in both hands looking straight down into it. Sergeant Carmody nodded sympathetically at Pat.

'Mr Forman's right, Miss. And if I were you two I'd go lie down for a bit as the doctor said. I'll stay here in case anyone's needed.'

Will tugged her up out of the chair. She didn't resist; with the need for her services suddenly gone, she let her resolve dwindle. In its place came the overwhelming weariness which she'd been keeping at bay only through will-power.

Will led her down the corridor, shoved open a door, led her over to the bed, sat her upon the edge of it then flicked on a lamp. It worked. The brightness was friendly to them both.

'Nothing more we can do,' he said quietly. 'Lie down, Pat.' He kissed her, eased her back and drew a blanket over her. That's the last thing she remembered.

But fear and terror are never opiates; they make their own variety of indelible impression. It can and often does return even in sleep to perpetuate fright and uncertainty. For the length of time Pat slept she didn't actually rest until the last three hours. By then the tensions had soporifically lessened, the nightmare had dwindled, and the demands of an exhausted body took over. That was when she got her real rest.

The body as a self-re-energizing unit has no equal in nature. When she awakened she was sore from the number of bruises she'd unconsciously absorbed throughout the previous twenty-four hours, and weak after her total relaxation; every muscle, nerve and sinew was flaccid. It was an effort to move at all nor did she immediately make the effort. She lay still, eyes closed again, savouring the rich luxury of complete relaxation.

It took a little time for her mind to re-live all that had transpired, to bring her up to the present moment. She knew by now the surgery was over. The child had either survived—or he had not survived. There was nothing she could do now which hadn't been done by others.

The chance of permanent brain injury, of some variety of mental lapse, had always been present in the back of her mind. Even if the operation had been a success and the boy had lived through it, not for several days, perhaps, would they be able to ascertain whether the pressures had in any way damaged the brain itself.

She went back in thought to the books she'd read on brain damage. None had left her with any hope of total recovery although nearly all had given an assurance that people who'd survived could be taught good and useful trades.

She let her mind drift back to Will Forman. She wondered if he'd got some rest too. He'd actually needed it more than she had. She recalled his gentle kiss a moment before she'd fallen asleep, and smiled softly.

Someone striding down the corridor towards her room brought her eyes open again. She thought it might be Will, she didn't know his stride yet. It wasn't; the person turned off into one of the other little rooms. At least she doubted that he'd have overlooked her if it had been Will.

The brightness bothered her. She reached to switch off the lamp and found that it wasn't lighted. She looked past where a closed window and light curtain broke an otherwise undisturbed run of tan wall, and saw something she'd almost forgotten. Sunshine!

She was annoyed that the curtains shut it out. Moving at last, she touched the floor, saw that her legs were bare and paused to consider this phenomenon. She had no recollection at all of removing either shoes or stockings.

With a little shrug she stood up, felt the little aches, moved across to draw the curtain and was nearly blinded by sunshine.

Steam was rising from the soggy world on every hand. There were no clouds in a pale blue sky so far as she could see, most of the water had disappeared and when she raised the window a bit she distinctly heard the high cry of children at play somewhere in the middle distance.

She stood with sunshine beating against her, feeling its life-giving warmth, more aware of it than she'd ever been before. The drowsiness vanished completely, the aches seemed to atrophy in sunshine. She felt nearly normal. It was almost as though she hadn't travelled through the kind of

Purgatory Dante had imagined.

She went across to her door, peeked out, saw no one and swiftly sought the bathroom. There, another window admitted blessed golden warmth. She bathed, brushed her hair, ruefully considered her rumpled dress, slipped back to her room and caught the distant, tantalizing aroma of frying bacon.

She didn't glance at her wristwatch until locating both shoes and stockings, she bent to put them on. It was nine in the morning.

She straightened up to consider this. They had left Harlham earlier than nine, of course, but on the other hand they'd crept very slowly across the intervening miles to reach their destination. Of course during the storm there was nothing to orient people to the hour of day or night, but that was gone now. She thought they must have reached the doctor's home about one or two o'clock in the afternoon.

She'd slept all night long! This was another, brand new day. She'd slept the remainder of the previous afternoon, all last night, and up until late this ensuing morning.

It took a bit of getting used to. She could

171

of course understand how she'd needed all that rest, but because she was not a person who normally dropped off for such long periods of time, she was surprised at herself.

Someone came with a small, swift step down towards her door. She'd finished dressing, stood and moved forward to look out. It was the doctor's wife looking as pert and immaculate as though she hadn't spent a long, gruelling time in surgery the day—or evening—before. She smiled at Pat.

'The others are threatening to eat it all up. I thought I'd look in on you.'

Pat stepped out, closed the door at her back and said, 'You've been so wonderfully kind.'

The older woman's assessing eyes missed nothing. 'And you've come back to the world of the living. I honestly don't see how you did it, Miss Brewster. You must come of extremely durable stock.'

Pat's smile wilted slightly. 'The operation...?'

'My husband is one of the best surgeons in the country. Thirty years ago he could have had any position in the land, but he chose general practice in the country.

Miss Brewster, his skill was equal to what needed doing.'

'The child is alive?'

'Alive? Miss Brewster, the child will be quite all right, given enough time for an adequate recovery.'

'No—internal damage?'

'None. Would you like to see the child?'

'No. He's probably resting. All I wanted to know was whether he'd come through it or not.'

'Quite.' The older woman smiled again. 'And now—breakfast?'

Pat nodded through a soft mist of unshed tears.

The doctor was not there, nor was Sergeant Carmody. He'd taken his lorry, Will told her, and headed on back to Harlham. Jeremy and Will were bathed, shaved, and as presentable as they could make themselves considering that they'd had to put on the same clothing again, dry though for a change.

A heavy, round-faced woman came through from either some rear pantry or kitchen to bring Pat's breakfast. The doctor's wife took her place at the head of the table. Pat had a feeling she couldn't have defined; she felt ecstatically alive and triumphant. Looking at Will's smooth-shaven, rugged profile as he ate, she wanted to reach over and touch him. He caught her watching him, raised his head a little, solemnly winked, then went back to eating.

The doctor's wife saw that and was not the least bit ruffled.

Jeremy Sloat seemed embarrassed when Pat smiled at him. He'd evidently been struggling to form some appropriate sentences without too much success. Nevertheless he lay aside his knife and fork, drew up in his chair and said, 'Miss Brewster, my son owes his life to you, to Mr Forman, Sergeant Carmody, and the doctor. I just don't know how to say how I feel towards the lot of you. I don't even know the proper words. But believe me, they're in m'heart. They'll always be there too, believe me, mum.'

Will smiled and the doctor's wife gazed at Jeremy as she said, 'That was well said, Mr Sloat. Very well said. We're not a demonstrative race, are we, but we feel as much and perhaps more than other races.'

Pat had privately and silently to agree with that.

CHAPTER SIXTEEN

She visited the sick child after breakfast, alone. He looked wan and wasted. His room was small, clean, and lighted by one very small bulb plugged directly into a wall socket.

When she emerged Jeremy was waiting. In sunlight he looked haggard and spent despite the rest he'd got. He said, 'The doctor had to go out on a call before I could talk to him. Miss Brewster, what do *you* think?'

She couldn't have said in any case for she hadn't been present at the operation, but neither was it any longer her place to say. 'I'm sure the doctor did exactly what had to be done. I haven't seen him either, Jeremy, but his wife told me your son came through it very well and will be all right given time to fully recover.'

Jeremy nodded. She'd told him nothing, but then what he wanted to know perhaps none of them could have told him. She asked if he had telephoned his wife. He had; he'd called her as soon as he'd awakened this morning. She said Pat's father had called the Sloat farm to find out whether Mrs Sloat'd had any word. That reminded Pat she'd forgotten to call home. She went at once to search for the telephone. When she found it Will was talking to someone. She arrived just as he finished speaking and stood thoughtfully listening. He saw her, winked, then held out the instrument.

'Your father.'

She took the telephone, heard her father's voice and poured out her story until, seeing Will's slight grin, she stemmed the flow of words so that her father could also speak. Afterwards, as she was putting the instrument back upon its cradle, Will said, 'Sergeant Carmody got back safely, your father said. Also, they've organized working parties to clean up the village. Oh yes—Catherine and her son are fine and your father has sent out inquiries about her husband. All we can do about that is keep our fingers crossed.'

He took her arm, led her out to the front of the house, opened the door and took her through into the sunshine. There, he dropped her arm, looked roundabout and said, 'I asked the sergeant to get word to John Weldon to come up here and take us home, if he can spare the time and providing the roads are open.' He looked at her. 'You look as lovely as ever. Damned if I understand how you do it.'

She took his hand and drew him out to the little front fence, opened the gate and walked on through into the steaming roadway where there was no traffic although they could hear cars and lorries on other nearby streets.

'Walk with me,' she said, keeping hold of him. 'Once, my father and I went to a horse race. After the race was run men walked the horses back and forth. My father said that was done to permit the animals to unwind; to get nerves and muscles back to normal, otherwise, if they'd simply stalled the horses, the poor things would have got stiff all over.'

'And you are likening me to a horse,' he said. 'Well, at least you made it a racehorse instead of a great plough-horse.'

'Both of us,' she corrected him, and felt his fingers tighten round her hand. 'How did it ever all come off right, Will?'

'Faith,' he promptly replied. 'Faith and

prayer. I couldn't honestly attribute it to much else.'

'Unless of course you were being modest,' she said, looking sideways at him. 'I would attribute it to faith, prayer—and your strong back.'

'For a woman you did rather well too, you know.'

'For a woman?'

'They aren't normally as physically rugged as men, are they?'

'No.'

'And you *are* a woman, Pat.'

'Why, thank you ever so much, Will.'

He strolled perhaps another ten feet with sunshine beating downward, then quietly said, 'Your sarcasm is inappropriate. In case you think you're too big or too old to be put across my knee, let me assure you you are wrong.'

She looked up and laughed. He smiled back. They strolled to the main roadway and stood a while watching motorized machines with scoop buckets on the front of them lifting loads of mud, debris, and pieces of freed paving stones, then dumping them into vehicles to be hauled away.

People were out, some examining their

buildings, some talking with friends, others just slowly strolling along surveying the wreckage, which was not as extensive as it would turn out to be over in Harlham, which had been directly in the centre of the storm.

She said, releasing his hand to brush back a heavy dark curl of hair, 'What does one do when one is no longer needed?'

'You won't have any answer to that,' he exclaimed, 'for quite a while. You'll be needed back in Harlham. But even if you weren't needed to splint arms and sew up gashes, I'd need you, Pat.'

She'd known of course that sooner or later they'd get round to discussing themselves. It was an inevitable aftermath of all they'd lived through together. But she'd begun to have an idea that under stress he had acted more gallantly towards her than he would have acted had there been no stress. She turned, quietly studied his leaned-down, weathered countenance and said, 'You don't need me, Will. I doubt very much whether you'll ever need a woman. You are perhaps the strongest man I've ever known.'

She started back. He fell in beside her saying, 'I thought we'd reached some kind of understanding last night. Of course no words were actually spoken, but then I've always had some idea that the language of love is silence.'

She paused. 'Love?'

He looked down at her. 'What else? I don't go round kissing girls, Pat. I assume you don't go about kissing men.'

She pulled at his sleeve. They started on again. Two laughing boys and a dog raced past. An elderly man with a coat buttoned to his chin despite the sunshine, nodded and briskly walked on past too.

He waited until there'd be no more interruptions then said, 'If it'll make you believe me I could have it tattoed on my chest in large letters: Pat I Love You.'

When she walked along saying nothing he looked askance, then fisted both hands, shoved them into trouser pockets and began to look a little stormy.

She could sense his changing mood. She didn't really know what to say. She knew how she felt and he'd made it plain enough how he felt, but it just wasn't that easy for her. Six years of bitterness couldn't be wiped out overnight.

Eventually, as they came close to the

doctor's establishment again, he said, 'Pat, just tell me one thing. About those kisses...'

That of course was the crux of the thing. She knew it. She also knew how she'd begun to feel towards him even before she'd kissed him back. She stopped, turned and lifted her eyes.

'The kisses were real,' she told him. 'They were sincere.'

'Then what's between us now?'

'Well,' she said, and faltered.

'You're not sure?'

'No. I'm sure enough, Will. I'm just afraid that's all.'

He drew forth his hands and spread them wide. 'Afraid of what? Of me, of yourself, or the past?'

'Perhaps a little of all three, Will. Can't I have a little more time?'

He dropped his arms. His wide shoulders slumped. 'All the time you'll need, love. But it doesn't make much sense to me. Last night—'

'Last night wasn't real for either of us, Will. We'd been living on nerve and little else too long.' She was very earnest with him now. 'Listen to me; I made one terrible mistake. I never want to do that again. The next time I want it to be real and permanent.'

He nodded, watching her expressions come and go, his gaze steady and reflective. 'All right, Pat. Take all the time you'll need. But I'll tell you one thing: *I* won't change. I've never been fickle and I'm too old to start being changeable now. I said I loved you. I want to marry you the best way—or the worst way—I know how. *I'll* be permanent, so all you've got to think out is whether or not *you* will be permanent.'

'What do you think, Will?'

His solemnity cracked a little, his lips softly lifted. 'I think you're searching yourself for something you'll never find. Look, you've been afraid for six years. What more proof do you need that you're not fickle? That this time you'll make it work?'

She smiled up at him. 'Thanks. You know, Will, you're a terrible hard person not to like.'

A racy little red car pulled in at the kerb. The elderly doctor climbed out briskly, stood looking at them a moment, followed their glances back to his car, and chuckled. 'Once in every man's life he should have one uninhibited love and one

182

extraordinary car...' He paused to glance houseward before completing his sentence. 'I was married rather young and therefore never had the chance for the uninhibited love—but this car has made up for it in many ways.' The chuckle died, the tough old face sobered. The doctor glanced at his watch, up at the sun, and said, 'Well, suppose you two come with me while I look in on our patient.' He turned, took one brisk step and halted. 'Oh, by the way, Miss Brewster, I've had it the back of my mind for some time now. Just never had a chance to come up to Harlham and suggest it to you? How would you like to move down here and be my full-time nurse?'

Pat stood like a statue for a moment. She just wasn't up to any decisions yet and now she'd had two very important ones thrown at her in less than a half hour.

The doctor, watching her face, turned and started towards the house. 'Never mind; it really wasn't the right time to ask you. But I'm so blasted rushed all the time. Have to overlook my lack of tact. But think about it, please think about it. Now let's look in on our patient.'

Jeremy was inside standing in the sitting-room with the doctor's wife. She looked relieved when her husband entered. 'Mr Sloat would like some information,' she said.

The doctor looked swiftly at Jeremy, made a snap-decision and jerked his head. 'Right enough Mr Sloat, come along.'

He led them briskly to the small room where the child lay. Obviously, his wife had only just left the room moments before because although the window was opened slightly the curtains were closed, and there was a small vase of fragrant flowers on a little marble-topped table which hadn't been there earlier.

The child's face was still puffy, his breathing shallow, his body limp and small beneath the covers. He showed very little sign of life and none of consciousness. Pat wondered a little about this since surgery had taken place some hours before but she said nothing as the doctor read the pulse, peered into the eyes and bent to closely examine the bandaging.

He said, 'Coming along very well, Mr Sloat. He's a tough child. Under circumstances such as he has had to endure, good health and a strong physique have stood him in good stead. As for your questions, believe me everything that needed doing has been done. It could have been accomplished under more completely sterile and perfectly professional conditions in hospital in London. My decision to do it all right here last night was based, as you'll appreciate, on the fact that delay would have been fatal, and that there was a very good chance he'd never have been able to reach the city anyway. Right?'

Jeremy nodded but Pat wasn't sure he even heard. He was standing slightly tipped forward seeming scarcely to breathe as he looked at his son in the bed. Pat could feel the anguish, the uncertainty, the terrible corrosive fear that was gnawing the man's spirit.

She put a light hand upon Jeremy's arm. He turned gradually. The doctor smiled at him radiating assurance.

'Good man,' said the doctor in a less brusque, less professional tone. 'Come to my study with me. Mr Sloat. I've exactly the right medicine for you.'

Pat and Will were followed to the door by the doctor's wife who closed the door between herself and them. She meant to remain yet a while with the sick child. Pat had already arrived at the conclusion that whether or not the medical pair had ever had children of their own, they were either gone now or had never been born, hence the motherly sympathy the doctor's wife manifested.

Pat took Will's hand and led him out into the sitting room where they were alone. She dropped his hand, turned and said, 'Until tomorrow when we're back in Harlham—is that too long a time to ask?'

He smiled gently. 'No. It's never been the time I've feared, Pat. It's been the answer.' He reached, she let him hold her and when he tipped up her face she didn't resist then either.

CHAPTER SEVENTEEN

The hardest decision to be made had to be made by Jeremy Sloat later in the day when John Weldon drove up outside the doctor's residence offering to take him back, along with Pat and Will.

Of course it was exclusively Jeremy's decision, and nothing would have changed that had any of the others sought to influence him. But none of them did;

even the doctor simply said the child obviously couldn't be moved, but he'd receive the best care and on that score Jeremy had nothing to worry about.

Pat could see the pull, could sense the anguish. Sloat owed allegiance in two places; at the bedside of his child and back at the farm with the rest of his family.

He of course ultimately made the only reasonable decision. He thanked the doctor, his wife, ran to look again at his small son, then came hurrying back so as not to delay the others and piled into John Weldon's asthmatic car with a promise to return as soon as he possibly could, and bring his wife.

The ride back was in a sense the climax to a triumph. Weldon told them their struggles were common community knowledge; that the village folk were agreed that both Pat and Will were local heroes.

He also told them government relief had been promised for those who had lost roofs or outbuildings or had suffered any other than the most minor loss. He twinkled a sly look at Will as she told them that.

'And it'll include your big glass window, I'm told. But were I in your boots, Will, seeing this is the second one in something less than two weeks, and seeing as they're terribly expensive—and uninsurable now in Harlham—I'd board it up solid.'

Their spirits were high, excepting Jeremy's which was understandable, but as they came within sight of Harlham even his moral was boosted by the sight of the village standing there as it had for centuries, under a winter sun, clear sky, and the kind of aura of permanence only British villages have.

He leaned back on the seat and quietly smiled. He had been born in Harlham. He would without much doubt die there. His father, grandfather and great-grandfather had all done the same. His children would in all probability live and die in Harlham. It was blending of people with their native environment in the fullest sense. It was something people felt and knew; it gave them strength, purpose, conviction, patience.

'A beautiful sight,' he told the others, watching the village lying peacefully in the sunshine with its grey roofs, its byways, roads and crooked ancient streets. 'We took the worst the storm could give and nothing's very changed.'

John Weldon had a pipe going. It had

soggy dottle and made bubbly sounds when he pulled on it. 'There'll be some change,' he said, 'because there'll be some repairing here and there. Jeremy, we didn't come through unscathed, you know. Esau lost the top of a shed. So did you.'

Weldon skirted a deep hole in the road, pointed ahead with his pipe and smiled as he said that while Jeremy was largely correct, there'd be no major changes because there'd been no major damage, nevertheless Harlham would never be quite as placid as it had been before.

'There might be another 'un come, you know. For all we know there may be a pattern working in weather conditions which'll put us in the path of the next storm as well.'

It wasn't a cheerful suggestion and the others, privately doubting, let the topic die then and there.

They drew up in front of Paul Brewster's place with sunshine playing over fresh washed ancient stone walls and shiny windows. Weldon waved off their expressions of thanks, told Jeremy he'd drive him on up to his farm and pulled away.

Pat's father came and stood in the doorway beaming. He'd shaved, bathed

189

and changed his clothing. He still looked tired but then he was not a young man; even sleep didn't always revitalize the elderly. He clasped Will's hand, opened his arms to his daughter, then led them inside to report that Gordon Johnson had gone home to get out his car and drive down to see the doctor by himself, now that he'd heard the roads were all accessible again, and he also reported that Catherine Everett and her baby were doing well.

'And Joan Eaton's been calling every hour or two. Seems her stomach pains have returned.' As he said this old Brewster waggled his head. 'Wretched malingerer,' he mumbled, leading them upstairs to Catherine's room.

The baby was sleeping. He'd fitfully clench a tiny fist or otherwise jerk a limb but he slept like a log and looked perfectly content. Catherine wanted to hear all about the nightmarish ride of the night before. Pat laughingly promised to tell her later, after she'd got them all some luncheon.

Will declined and left. He had his shop to look after, he told them, and promised to return later in the day or the following morning, depending on how much work he found awaiting him.

They parted at the front door without kissing or even touching hands, but their eyes communicated. Pat later on, after she'd cleaned up and was having the first quiet, restful moment in her own home for almost forty-eight hours, told her father Will wished to marry her.

He nodded without showing any undue elation. All he said was. 'He'll make you a fine husband. He's serious and practical and hard-working.'

She studied the old man's face. 'It will complicate things,' she said. 'For example he owns his own home and—'

'Wait a moment, Patience. You're very fortunate that he owns a home. Very few young marrieds nowadays are so lucky.'

'I didn't mean it that way, Father. I mean—I'll have to stop being the local nurse and I'll have to move out of here which will leave you alone.'

'Hah!' snorted the old man. 'Be a blessed change not having my house treated as a depot of some kind with people running in and out at all hours. Don't you worry about me living alone. Anyway, you'd not be moving out of the country you know. As for not being a nurse, after what I've seen lately I should imagine you'd like that.'

'They'll still need me, Father.'

'Will they now? And what were they doing before we came here? They had a nurse then and they'll have another after you've dropped it.' Old Brewster, committed to his argument, leaned a little to say, 'Patience, how many chances to marry *good* men do women get in their lifetimes? I'll tell you—if they're very fortunate perhaps two such chances. Otherwise just one. Now come along to the kitchen, I'm hungry and I'm sure Catherine also is.'

They didn't argue, actually, at any point in their discussion, but they certainly covered all pertinent angles with Pat taking the negative view and her father taking, if not the positive, then at least the hopeful viewpoint.

Later, they took some supper up to Catherine, then Frank and Joan Eaton called round shortly after eight at night. Not, as Pat feared the moment she saw who it was her father had admitted to the entry hall, to ask her to look at Joan and listen to her stomach grumble, but to ask almost breathlessly if Pat and her father had heard the latest rumour: There was another storm on its way from out over the North Sea, and it was thought to be worse than the previous storm.

Pat's father went to the wireless for confirmation. Exasperatingly, all he got was music, someone selling something, or the droning, un-funny voice of a comedian. He ultimately had to wait until the half-hour break in programming to seek out a newscaster.

There was no mention of a storm coming. There was some comment, mostly statistical, on the recent storm, but no prognostications respecting future storms. In fact, when he eventually got a weather report, it was said the idyllic calm weather would continue through the balance of the current week while the thirty-day forecast was definitely favourable.

He became immensely annoyed, telling Pat there definitely were advantages to some of the painful but minor tortures used in mediaeval times against rumour-mongers and spreaders of false tales.

Gordon Johnson came round shortly before bedtime to bring Pat a very lovely cashmere cardigan and her father a brown bottle of some hallowed whisky. When Pat mentioned something about their being rules against gratuities, Lawyer Johnson raised his eyebrows in mock surprise and said, 'What gratuities, might I ask? My dear, this is a present to a lovely woman from a great admirer. Believe me, it has nothing to do with gratitude. As for the whisky—didn't we nearly drink up your father's private supply last night? All I'm doing here is repaying in small part what I owe.'

After Johnson had left Pat said she was going to retire, that she was exhausted. If Will rang, her father was to tell him she'd ring him in the morning.

Old Brewster kissed her cheek, saw her up the stairs, went into his tiny study to read a bit, and later on, after peeking in on Catherine and her child and finding both soundly sleeping, he slipped out and headed for the Coach and Four.

John Weldon was at his bar, and, it being well within licensing hours, there were nearly a dozen men in the pub, but while Esau Gibbon was on hand Jeremy Sloat was not. Esau was wearing wellingtons. Frank Eaton was there and shortly after Paul Brewster entered, Will Forman also arrived.

It was, smiling John Weldon said, just

194

like it had been before they'd ridden out their second storm, and he was happy to report that to his knowledge, while there had been damage, none terribly extensive, there had not been a single life lost.

'You can't say yet,' exclaimed Esau Gibbon. 'Jeremy's boy's still critically ill.'

Weldon's smile winked out as he nodded, evidently having forgotten that. Forman told them gruffly from a stool next to old Brewster at the bar, what the doctor had said; that the child would in all probability recover without any serious after-effects.

They drank to that.

Weldon confided he had a cellar full of water and was considering the procurement of fish so as to add an additional inducement to his customers. That opened the way for considerable garrulous comment on damage, experiences, fears and adventures during the recent storm.

Someone said a team of people was to arrive in Harlham to inoculate everyone against typhoid or something like that. This took them all off on a fresh tangent, some favouring the idea, others dead against it on the grounds that Harlham needed no outsiders, particularly blasted do-gooders, but of course this was the reactionary element; everyone knew the government had only their best interests at heart.

Paul Brewster said, after his second glass of beer, that whatever ensued the villagers would doubtless survive it having just come through probably the worst storm in local if not national history, but he, being addicted to the resolute resourcefulness of an earlier generation of Britons, rather felt what they all needed now was privacy to re-order their lives, and not the confounded meddling of a lot of educated nincompoops.

This statement caused a pause while everyone who knew old Brewster had been a university lecturer, gazed reflectively at Pat's father as though he'd just uttered something treasonable.

Will Forman raised his glass. Others did likewise. Old Brewster appeared not to notice this vote of confidence although he smiled when he looked at Will.

'I wonder who'll be our next resident nurse,' he said quietly as the others turned back to their talk.

Will looked at him without comment. Old Brewster leaned a little. John Weldon who'd been standing close, was called away. Brewster said, 'I've made a lifelong study of the human response. It is an absorbing subject not ordinarily studied except by military and advertising men.'

Will sat listening and gazing upon the older man with thoughtful eyes. He knew old Brewster well enough to realize that although he might take ten minutes to get to the point, when he spoke out he usually had something worthwhile to say.

'Advertising psychologists exploit people's fears or hopes, or their current anxieties. They make them pay for whatever product they are trying to sell. Military men, using fundamentally the same techniques, equate everything with tactics. Now if I were a young man in love I dare say I'd do something along those lines myself.'

Will said, 'You mean you'd press the attack?'

Brewster beamed. 'Quite perceptive,' he said. 'Of course if the lady were asleep I'd wait until morning, but I most certainly wouldn't wait a bit longer, and I'd also be aggressive. In a moderate manner you understand. But I'd permit little time for a lot of ridiculous doubts and fears to shoot me down.'

Will slowly smiled. 'Good strategy,' he agreed, drank down his stout, dropped a coin on top of the bar, winked at old Brewster and departed.

CHAPTER EIGHTEEN

For Pat the day after her return home was a day to cherish. She'd scarcely finished feeding Catherine and tending to the needs of Catherine's child when she was informed by telephone that Catherine's husband was making anxious inquiries by long-distance telephone concerning his wife.

Pat took the call, introduced herself to Catherine's husband, told him what had happened, that his wife and son were fine, and asked what his condition was. He seemed mildly surprised at that, saying that he'd been ashore on the south coast of England where they'd got no unseasonably bad weather at all.

Pat hastened upstairs to put Catherine's mind at rest and to leave her the little Japanese radio. She then returned to the kitchen to clean up their breakfast dishes and didn't hear her father enter the room until he said, 'Good morning, Nurse.'

It was another of those beautiful mornings, bright with winter sunshine. As her father noted, although Britain's average temperature left something to be desired among natives of warmer places as well as Britons who'd been to more lush and tropical lands, when the sun was unobscured by clouds or the promise of a shower, there was no clearer sky, no more fragrant air, and no more dazzling beauty than could be found in an English countryside.

She felt better than she'd felt for days. In fact she thought in her six years at Harlham she'd never felt so light-hearted and thoroughly happy.

She couldn't have explained that sensation. Even when her observant father commented on it, mentioning the brightness of her glance, the lightness of her step, she could only smile saying it was relief; that after a full, undisturbed night's rest at home in her own bed, she had awakened that morning without a single peril in the offing.

He ate the breakfast she got him, said very little until he was finished, then, glancing at his watch as though his life were still ordered by being in the lecture room on time, said he'd some business to attend to and left the house.

He hadn't been gone fifteen minutes when Will came in. She didn't consider the possibility of them passing each other in the road. In fact she didn't even consider the feasibility of collusion between her father and Will Forman.

She took him through the house to see Catherine, then out into the rose garden where the storm had caused some damage, although not very much because some previous owner had erected a brick wall to the west and north, evidently so motivated because these were the directions of prevailing winds. To the south and east the garden was protected by some somewhat flattened bushes and immense, low trees which did not appear to have lost so much as a limb.

She got stakes and twine and set him to tying up the rose bushes which had fallen. She told him about Catherine's husband. When he asked if she'd rung up to see how Jeremy's child was coming along, she shook her head. She'd been partly afraid to, she said, and partly unwilling to bother the doctor who would be very busy for the next day or two. She then said that Jeremy had probably rung up, as though Jeremy were there with them and Will could turn and ask him about the child. He simply gazed at her, went back to tying rose bushes and said nothing for a while.

It became quite warm. He shed his coat, hung it on a tree limb and returned to work. This wasn't quite what he'd had in mind when he'd called round, but on the other hand he'd promised her all the time she needed to make up her mind and doggedly adhered to that now, when one word might have led her into saying what was in her mind and heart.

She got them a cup of tea later on. They sat in a sunny window seat to sip it. In the circumstances it was difficult to imagine that two nights before they'd been groping through a howling horror.

She mentioned the village, saying she hadn't yet been able to walk through it. He replied that there was nothing to see, really; that without any major destruction all she'd see would be people cleaning up debris in the road, deposited there in muddy heaps wherever receding floodwater had left it.

'Aerials mostly. Won't be much telly viewing for a while.' He finishd the tea but kept hold of his cup and saucer.

'Your shop?' she asked.

'All right, love. Not much more damage than after the window gave way again. I'd anticipated it somewhat this time. Of course things got soaked and whatever was in paper cartons was a mess, but otherwise it's not too bad.'

They sat a moment gazing at one another. She finally reached, took his cup, set both cups upon the table at her side and said, 'I can't really imagine why you want to marry me, Will. You could do much better.'

He relaxed a little, now that his purpose in being in the window seat with her was out in the open. He also smiled. 'Well you see I haven't much time to look round for another girl, what with having to clean up the shop again and go over my roof to see if any slates have been swept away.'

She caught his smile and returned it. 'I'm no dewy-eyed girl.'

'Twenty-four years old,' he said, and wagged his head dolorously. 'But I must say you're well preserved for a person your age.'

'And a sceptic, Will.'

He lost the smile. 'A sceptic? Hardly, Pat. A sceptic is someone who becomes resigned very easily. You never once became resigned on the lorry ride, nor before that when the world seemed about to blow away. Now if you'd said a cynic...'

'That too, perhaps, Will,' she said rising to go to the kitchen with their empty cups. 'And a bit of a coward.'

'What about?'

'You don't have to ask that, you already know what about. Us.'

He unwound slowly to stand facing her. 'We've been over all this. The only thing I haven't said is that if you'll work half as hard to insure the success of our marriage as you've worked so far to make yourself fear it, love, it couldn't possibly fail.'

She smiled softly. 'Will you tie up the rest of the roses while I look in on Catherine? She might be hungry.'

He said, 'I've a better idea. I'll carry her down here to the window-seat. Let her see beauty and feel sunshine.'

She recoiled instinctively from such a

radical suggestion saying, 'Oh; I don't know, Will...'

He hooked his arm through hers and swept her along upstairs with him as he said, 'I once read a book that claimed Red Indians had children in the morning and were up and about doing their ordinary household work in the afternoon.'

'That's commendable but Catherine isn't a Red Indian,' she answered as she went upstairs with him and didn't really object when he offered to carry Catherine down to the window-seat in fact, when she saw the way Catherine's face lighted up—as much she suspected over the prospect of being in Will's arms as being taken downstairs—she consented to carry the baby.

When he lifted Catherine he looked surprised. 'I thought you'd weigh more,' he said.

She blushed. 'Well, I did several days ago, Mr Forman.'

They went down the stairs and again Pat held her breath but Will seemed remarkably sure-footed despite the fact that his visibility was somewhat impaired by the girl clinging to him.

He carefully put Catherine down on one of the seats in the sunny window. Pat shielded the baby from direct sunlight. He burrowed against her making soft snuffling sounds, tiny hands kneading her arms. She looked up to find Will standing motionless looking at her with an odd expression in his eyes. The moment he saw her watching he said he'd get back to work tying up the rose bushes. Before he went he asked Catherine how long her husband had been a seaman, and whether he was in the Merchant Navy or the Royal Navy.

'Merchant Navy, Mr Forman. I think I heard someone say you once served too.'

'I may go back to it,' he said to Catherine and keeping his back to Pat who sat straight up on her seat. 'It's actually an interesting life. Some men make careers of it.'

'Not my husband,' pouted Catherine. 'I don't think a man with a family has the right to be away all the time, do you?'

'Definitely not,' replied Will, still not looking at Pat. 'But you see I have no family so it'd be all right for me.'

Pat began to get an inkling what this was all about. He was reaching her through the younger girl. She even thought of a retort, but in the end she didn't utter it.

'Someday you'll marry, Mr Forman,'

Catherine exclaimed very earnestly. 'When the right girl comes along.'

'How will I know her?'

'You'll know her the same as she'll know you. It'll be like—like something you've never experienced before. Rather like a charge of electricity.'

'Well, but it has to be mutual, doesn't it?' he asked still not looking round.

'It will be,' responded Catherine, with no inkling she was being used as a foil between Will and Pat. 'She'll know too.'

'And if she doesn't feel anything...?'

'Then she's not the right one, Mr Forman.'

He finally turned, his face perfectly blank but his eyes ironically twinkling at Pat. 'I'll need a bit more string for the rest of the rose bushes, Miss Brewster.'

She handed Catherine the baby and went out to the kitchen. He was teasing her, deliberately tormenting her. There was another ball of string in the pantry. It hadn't been unrolled. There was a slip of paper glued to it with a trade-name. She took the ball and started back to the sitting-room, then, on the spur of the moment, went in search of a pen, wrote four tiny words across the slip of paper and finally returned to the room where he was waiting, talking to Catherine.

She handed him the ball of string, pointed out to him a bush which was drooping near the wall of the garden, and gave him her most engaging smile.

He flipped the ball of string, caught it and said, 'Catherine, do you suppose the man who marries Pat Brewster would be dominated by a shrew? All she's thinking of just now is having her blasted roses tied up.'

Catherine's eyes suddenly widened. It had belatedly dawned on her, evidently, that there was byplay and undercurrent here. She blushed for some reason and shook her head.

'I think Miss Brewster is very stunning.'

'She could still be a shrew, couldn't she?'

'Oh no, Mr Forman. Not Miss Brewster.'

He almost laughed at the solemn look accompanying those words. He and Pat exchanged a look, then he turned and strode out into the garden. As he went he called over his shoulder to say he wasn't convinced Miss Brewster mightn't be a vixen. Although his back was to them, both girls guessed he was laughing. Pat had been silent up to now.

She opened the window, leaned out and said to Catherine loudly enough for him to hear. 'There is nothing quite as annoying as an opinionated man.' She might have added to that except that Catherine suddenly leaned back hugging her child as Will turned and strode swiftly back to the house holding the ball of string.

Pat stood up quickly, her heart pounding. She knew by the look on his face he'd been able to make out the four words on the label, each one of which had been capitalized.

'I WILL MARRY YOU.'

He came into the room and stopped, handed Catherine the ball of string as though it were responsible for what he intended doing, then he reached for Pat with both arms. She went quickly to him.

Catherine gazed quizzically at the ball of string, saw the four inked words, studied them closely, then uttered a little squeak of comprehension.

By then Will and Pat were locked in a long, long kiss.

CHAPTER NINETEEN

When Pat's father returned later for lunch with a parcel of groceries, Catherine was sitting in the parlour holding her son. He stopped to stare. The last he'd known she'd still been bed-ridden upstairs. He set aside the groceries and stepped silently into the room.

She said, speaking in a normal tone of voice. 'He sleeps like a log, Mr Brewster. People walking about and talking don't bother him at all.' She looked at her child a moment. 'And I've decided on a name.'

'Oh? Something traditional I trust, Catherine.'

'William Paul.'

Old Brewster thought that over. 'William Paul. No doubt William is for Will Forman, who brought you in out of the storm, as it were, but Paul...'

'For you.'

Old Brewster blushed. He looked round as though Pat might have overheard. He said, 'But of course I'm terribly flattered, child, only actually I didn't do a thing. My daughter—'

'The next one, if it's a girl, Mr Brewster, will be named after Patience Brewster. But this is a boy. And you held the candle and read from the medical book during delivery. You were almost as important as Mr Forman at a very critical time. I'm only trying to show my deep gratitude, Mr Brewster.'

He dropped down beside the chair, patted Catherine's shoulder and said softly, 'I'm terribly pleased, child, undeservedly honoured. But doesn't it seem the lad should be named for his father?'

'Herodotus?'

Old Brewster blinked. 'That's his father's name?'

Catherine nodded. 'He doesn't use it. He calls himself Harold.'

'Yes, of course. Fine old Saxon name. But how on earth did your husband get a name like Herodotus?'

'His father read of this Herodotus. I think he was a Greek historian. His father said the Greek Herodotus was also one of the most wise men who ever lived.'

Old Brewster couldn't dispute that fact,

but he could have questioned hanging such a name on anyone in the present age. Still, he was respectful of the admiration Catherine's father-in-law had shown and merely murmured something to the effect that Herodotus was indeed a great historian and noble philosopher, but on the other hand Harold seemed a more appropriate name.

He asked where Pat was. Catherine told him she and Will were outside. She then gazed doubtingly at old Brewster, started to speak, changed her mind and simply suggested he go out to them.

Paul Brewster was well into his sixties; all his mature years had been spent in a field where men have to be dense as granite not to discern things others have thought but not spoken of aloud. He rose somewhat stiffly, patted Catherine's shoulder, turned and went back to take the groceries into the kitchen. Then he peered out of a window where he could see the entire garden. Pat and Will were standing close together in the shadow of the trees. He didn't have to go out to them; he didn't even have to be told what had transpired in his absence.

He rummaged for the bottle Gordon

Johnson had brought, filled a small glass, raised it in a silent and unobserved salute to the lovers, and dropped the whisky straight down. There was nothing like a drink of good whisky, alone, to assuage the inevitable sense of loss a father felt when he could see the way his daughter was gazing at a young man, even when the father had fervently wished for this very thing to happen for a very long time.

The liquor helped for what he had to do next; go out to them. He got as far as the entry hall when the telephone rang. Because his thoughts were so distant from anything so mundane he gave a little start and half turned as though expecting the instrument to be alive.

It was John Weldon calling from his home over the Coach and Four. He asked for Pat, saying he'd come down with a frightful fever and couldn't get out to see the doctor. Brewster said he'd tell her and replaced the telephone, turned and walked straight out into the garden.

'John Weldon's calling for you,' he said, nodding to them both as he approached. 'Just telephoned to say he has a frightful fever.'

Pat stiffened, gazing straight at her

father. The first fear, of course, was some variety of epidemic following in the wake of the storm. There were Royal Engineers and volunteer units of local people taking care of the debris, keeping all drains un-plugged, working hard to prevent anything like this happening, but polluted water was one thing that always loomed large after any savage storm, despite the best efforts of everyone.

She was holding Will's hand as she turned back to say, 'You must come with me.'

She'd heard of the inoculation team, but only as a rumour. No one had contacted her respecting it, which would certainly have been the case had any such team arrived in Harlham.

Will said, 'If it's typhoid or anything like that I should imagine the thing to do at once would be to isolate whoever is infected to prevent the spread to those such as Catherine's baby who'd have no resistance.'

She squeezed his fingers and tugged. She told her father she'd ring him straightaway if it turned out to be anything dangerous.

They didn't go back through the house although, after passing around to the front, alongside the house, she ran back to pick up a few things she might need, then hastened out to meet him again.

It seemed so incongruous on a beautiful sunny day for death to be stalking their village. When she mentioned several possibilities, he hung back about agreeing with her.

'Ptomaine poisioning,' he said. 'Perhaps nothing worse than influenza. After all, most of us got wet and chilled. I should imagine this would be about the right incubation period for some virus infection.'

She wasn't soothed at all. 'Suppose it *is* an epidemic.'

'Then all the children should be either inoculated against it or sent away until it's run its course. But I think the greatest peril would be for someone to start a rumour.'

She looked at him as they briskly strode along. He hadn't meant *she'd* start any such rumour, of course, but his words had carried weight. She thought of Joan Eaton and Jeremy Sloat's wife, both inveterate gossips. He was right, of course; if any such talk started now, it would spread like wildfire. By nightfall one half of Harlham would be abed, the other half would be fleeing.

When they reached the Coach and Four Weldon called to them that the front door was unlocked and to come upstairs. They entered, Will leading the way. They were both very grave and unsmiling when they stepped into Weldon's small, cluttered parlour—and were greeted by over a dozen grinning faces.

John Weldon, wearing an excellent Harris Tweed jacket, said loudly: 'Surprise!'

The others all joined in. There was a rich smell of food and a number of handsomely labelled bottles stood discreetly at hand on tables. Will stood and owlishly looked around. Jeremy Sloat and his wife were there. Even Sergeant Carmody, looking flushed and very pleased, thrust out a strong hand.

'I can see by your face it *was* a surprise,' he said, pumping Will's hand, then dropping it to turn to Pat. 'It's a fine town you have here, Miss Brewster; fine people.'

Pat looked weakly at Will. He was making a slow, sick smile as the people crowded up offering glasses to them both. Weldon said, 'A bit early for celebrating, I realize, but most of 'em can't stay long, they'll have to get back to their jobs.

215

Anyway, we wanted you both to know how much the community appreciates all you did the other night.'

Jeremy's wife slipped over, took Pat's arm and led her out of the crush of people where several other women including Joan Eaton, were waiting with fruit-flavoured drinks.

They had been working all the morning to arrange all this Pat was told, and had been fearful lest some word of it leak out. Pat assured them in a voice deepened by relief that until she'd walked in the parlour door she'd had no idea at all it was a surprise party.

Will had a drink with Sergeant Carmody, who said his outfit had been withdrawn but that the people of Harlham had reached him by telephone and he'd got leave to drive back.

Will also had a drink with Jeremy who told him the doctor said Jeremy's son was coming along famously. 'Talking a blue streak, he is, which is normal for the lad, and there's nothing amiss with his memory, which was what the missus and I feared.'

'When can you bring him home?' Will asked.

'Next week.' Jeremy's smile dwindled, he looked round where his wife and the other women were surrounding Pat. 'A fine girl,' he said. 'The way John Weldon put it fits best. He said she wasn't just beautiful, which she obviously is, but she's got a real head on her shoulders, for a woman.'

Will smiled; he had no difficulty at all believing those were Weldon's exact words. He knew John well enough, knew his private opinion of women in general; knew that lifelong bachelorhood had made a mild yet confirmed misogynist out of John Weldon.

The luncheon was ample, hot and altogether delightful. People spilled over into the small dining-room, their voices rising in laughter and anecdote. Esau Gibbon was there dressed in a suit that fitted a bit tightly across the shoulders, his weathered, honest red face sticking above the tight collar and necktie.

It was early evening before Gibbon and Jeremy had to get back to their farms for the chores. Sergeant Carmody had to also take his leave. It was improbable any of them would see him again, so the handshakes were a little firmer, which was the way with men who didn't know the words—and wouldn't have used them if they'd found them—for sealing a friendship born in direct adversity. All their lives had touched in a dark night for all of them; none would ever forget whether they met again or not.

It was later when Pat and Will also departed. John had to first recite how the entire plot was hatched in his pub, and how everyone had pitched in to make it a gala little celebration. Pat kissed his cheek and John got as red as a beet.

Afterwards, together arm in arm in the winter dusk, Will told her old John probably wouldn't wash that side of his face.

'But,' she retorted, strolling along close to him, 'he's notorious for having a very low regard for women.'

'Women perhaps—but not of *one woman.*'

She hugged his arm saying, 'That's the greatest compliment ever given me, Will.'

He moved along perhaps fifty feet then dryly said, 'Well, not exactly. The greatest compliment was when I asked you to marry me.'

She was startled for a second, then

glossed it over by giving his arm another hard squeeze as she said, 'That goes without saying.'

There was a sliver of yellow-ivory up in the sky amid a scatter of blue-white diamonds. The night was still, the village lighted, the smell of smoke permeated the calm air, and somewhere a dog barked happily.

He took her by his shop and showed her the extent of storm damage. He'd boarded up the shattered front window and said he thought he'd have the window replaced, but that he'd also take some advice he'd been receiving on every hand and have a carpenter in to install stout wooden shutters.

They started back towards her father's house. He remembered something and said, 'I've got to get that ball of string back from Catherine.' His eyes were smiling down at her. 'I'm going to save that to show our grandchildren. I doubt very much if any woman ever before agreed to marry someone precisely in that manner.'

She laughed. It was a rich contralto sound in the soft night. Then she said, 'I wouldn't have guessed in my most delirious moment the night before last things would have turned out as they have.'

He stopped her in the centre of the pavement, turned her by the shoulders and kissed her. It was a gentle, affectionate kiss, the kind an admiring husband would bestow upon a happy wife, not the kind of kiss a lusting lover would have ever given a girl he was pursuing.

Afterwards she sighed, lay her head upon his shoulder, and finally felt the last of her doubts and fears melt away.

An elderly gentleman cleared his throat in a nearby doorway, then cheerily smiled as they resumed their way, nodding, and they both nodded back, also smiling. The elderly gentleman watched them out of sight, still smiling.

CHAPTER TWENTY

Will called the following afternoon to take Pat down to his building, which had the chemist's shop on the ground floor and a flat above.

It was a sturdy building flanked to

the west by Morton's the draper's and haberdasher's, and to the east by a jeweller's. Some previous owner had spent a considerable sum having the front of the building modernized. All the other buildings roundabout still retained their stone walls while Will's building had been refaced to appear a bit more up to date.

When Pat commented on this, Will pulled a long face. 'That's why the blasted window broke both times. Look at the other shops hereabouts. They not only have no large windows, but the ones they have are protected by shutters. Not my modern window; it wasn't supposed ever to see a bad storm.'

Upstairs in the flat the modernizing had been more functional. The rooms weren't large but there actually were three bedrooms, which wasn't common, and the dining-room and sitting-room were both very light and airy.

'Americanized,' was the way Will described it, and she knew he was watching for her reaction.

She thought it a handsome place, and whether the concept of greater space through the use of windows was American or not, she liked it and said so.

221

He led her over to where it was possible to see the road they'd crossed during the storm. She could even discern the entrance to that little alleyway down which they'd struggled. It all seemed ages ago. When he pointed to the wall of a distant building and said that was where he'd eased her down after she'd been struck on the head, she said it was like a bad dream, all of it.

He took her downstairs and out to the back. She smiled, for he had a tiny garden out there. It showed enthusiastic if not very knowledgeable care. There were three rose bushes, some snowdrops, and a spindly little tree that seemed to have been neglected until very recently and now, pruned and fertilized, was making a gratified come-back.

'My acreage,' he said, and laughed. 'I don't know why I bother.'

She thought she knew. He wasn't old enough yet nor domesticated enough to be willing at the day's end to take a book to the sitting-room and contentedly read. He still had the urge towards physical labour in him. He was strong and healthy and physically sound. His kind of man was slow to accept the blandishments of sedentary existence. Time would take care of that.

She asked about the little tree. It had been out there when he'd bought the property. The first year he hadn't paid any attention to it. The second year, seeing it slowly dying, he'd decided to spade up around it and see that it got properly tended.

'And of course, as those things work out,' he told her, 'before I knew it I got the rose bushes.'

'To keep the tree company?'

His eyes twinkled back at her. 'Something like that. I'd come out here in the evenings and scratch up the ground, pull weeds and... Well, you know, you have a garden too. After a bit I decided to make this my refuge, so I had to plant things. The old British urge, you know: If one sees a bit of untended ground, put it into some kind of production.'

They strolled back through the shop. He left her briefly to run upstairs for his coat. She went to the doorway and leaned there. It would be a tame existence, she thought, bringing up a family upstairs, tending their postage-stamp garden, perhaps from time to time helping him in the shop.

The kind of existence offering security, affection, protection, perhaps satisfaction in all the ways a woman needed to be satisfied.

For some it wouldn't be enough; they'd need travel, excitement, perhaps even danger, to negate ineffable boredom, but for Pat Brewster it was a sweet thought, being loved and cherished, having their children, perhaps each summer going to the Continent for a week or two but always coming back to Harlham.

A woman needed to belong, to have her own niche which was important to others as well as to herself. Her first love had offered her none of these tame things; in fact what he'd offered had been a day-by-day existence, moving from city to city, avoiding the country villages, even towns because there wasn't enough money in the smaller places.

He'd been a strikingly handsome man with bold, passionate blue eyes and crisp fair hair. But he'd been born ten centuries too late; he was a wild Saxon with a need for crises in his everyday life. She'd finally torn herself loose from him for exactly that reason. She'd wanted something much tamer. But he'd come back to twist the knife in her heart. She'd got weak for a while, then he laughed and called her an easy score, a soft bit of fluff, a poor excuse for a red-blooded woman, and he'd left.

He'd been as fair as Will Forman was dark. They were the same size, the same build, except that Will was heavier of bone, larger of hand and more cat-like in movement.

They could have been of the same stock, doubtless they were, but there was a solidness, a taciturn durability to Will the other man had totally lacked. Will laughed and smiled but he did those things rarely. He had a sense of humour, a sense of proper timing, a capacity to inspire faith, but he didn't work hard at any of those things, he didn't push himself forward. He never forced an issue when patience was required.

There could be no doubt of it, Will Forman was by far the better of the pair of them, but then she'd never doubted that. Nor had she ever doubted her own capacity to love. What had troubled her had been the gnawing doubt about men generally. Could they appear one thing, then turn out to be altogether different?

She still believed that by and large this

was possible. What she *didn't* believe was that Will Forman was that kind of chameleon. She had seen him angry, exhausted, fearful, cheerful, just about every way a woman would ever see any man, and he'd rung true each time; had been predictably uncomplicated, honest and resolute.

She sighed, watched the sunset, and when he came striding along she looked up into his face with a smile, then they strolled on out into the soft-falling early evening.

Harlham had once possessed a restaurant. It no longer did, but there were restaurants in nearby villages if one cared to make the drive. Will made the suggestion but Pat said she'd settle for Weldon's pub where a limited assortment of pre-packaged tidbits were always available.

That's where they went, but because of licensing hours weren't admitted to the pub until they'd visited with John Weldon for a while first. He was very strict on that score and always had been. But he was amiable when they came along, discussed the lack of a restaurant which he abhorred, as well he might being a single man, and told them he thought he might even take a chance and open one himself, in conjunction with the pub possibly, someday.

They discussed a number of things while waiting for opening time. The only time there was an interruption was when a Jaguar pulled up outside, and some people alighted, and talked together before deciding to ask for accommodation for the night.

Pat strolled outside to watch the settling shadows mantle Harlham. She was at peace in her heart and mind. She must have looked that way to the tourists because they pleasantly smiled as they trooped inside to register for rooms.

She knew, the moment Will came out to her, she looked that way to him because he felt for her fingers, squeezed them and stood with his wide shoulders to the front of the building at her side, silent and also watching the shadows deepen into the night.

She said, 'If we could see the future it might help, mightn't it?'

He didn't think so. 'If folks knew what lay round the corner they'd either break their necks getting there, or break them dashing in the opposite direction. More the latter than the former I suppose, since from what most of us know of the past makes it appear improbable Nirvana is on ahead.'

She laughed at his solemn look, 'Then why get married, Will?'

He was rueful about that. 'Instinct I suppose, to be awfully candid about it. But that wouldn't be all of course.' He thought a bit then added more. 'I'd much prefer having company in my triumphs as well as my failures.' His eyes lit up softly. 'You know the old saying about misery liking company.'

'You're so romantic,' she chided him.

He grinned. 'Well, I keep trying. You've got to give me credit for that. Perhaps after a few years I'll be passable at it.' He squeezed her fingers again, looked round, saw the lights on inside the pub and started to say something. But looking at her profile, the words died. She was very beautiful in the soft-sad light of the winter evening. Something about her tugged at him, held him silent and still at her side.

A dirty car pulled up out in front, stopped with a lurch and Gordon Johnson climbed out. He had his broken arm in an elegantly clean cast. He squinted to make certain who was standing over there away from the light, then walked up to them, his florid countenance shiny from soap and water.

'What the deuce are you two doing out here? Come along; I'll be delighted to buy a round.'

Pat asked about the arm. Johnson glanced at it almost as though it belonged to someone else. 'Done up fit and proper. The doctor said it'd been set right the first time.' Johnson, evidently suddenly thinking of something, looked hard at Will. 'Mind telling me where you learnt to set broken bones?'

'I thought I told you the other night. While I was a seaman.'

'Yes. Well, there's got to be more to it than that. A lot of men are seamen but they can't do what you did.'

Will smiled slightly. 'I was an exceptional seaman,' he said. 'Now you'd better get inside before the tourists drink the place dry.'

Johnson's attention perked up. 'Tourists? Probably came down to see the wreckage after our famous storm, eh?' He dutifully marched off, a thick, rather shapeless man with a confident walk, an almost brusque manner, and a thrust to his head that put Pat in mind of a bull-dog.

She turned. 'Will, where *did* you learn to set bones?'

He looked at her. 'I've just told Gordon. You were standing here listening.'

'All right, love,' she said softly. 'Don't tell me.'

He watched her turn away and look straight in front of her again. 'All right. I was a medical orderly for a brief stretch in the army. Later, I went on a short medical course before entering the Merchant Navy and became a seagoing medical orderly—whatever you choose to call it. Nothing more mysterious or romantic about any of it.'

She nodded, satisfied. 'You don't like to talk about yourself, do you?'

He shrugged. 'It would make very dull conversation. I've ridden out a few storms, seen something of war—in foreign ports you understand and from a respectable distance—but delivering Catherine's baby was truly the most adventurous thing I ever attempted. I don't mind admitting that afterwards I shook like a leaf.'

She appreciated his inherent reticence to talk about himself. She also knew that over the years everything he'd ever done would come out. And she possessed the virtues of her christian name.

She turned to peer through the pub window. There were several people inside, their backs to the window. The tourists no doubt, since she didn't recognize any of them.

He was still holding her hand. 'Shall we go and ask Gordon to honour that pledge?'

She stepped forth. At once he turned with her. Their shoulders touched, their hands loosened. He freed himself and reached. She didn't even look first as she came up against him there in the winter dusk.

'I love you very much,' he whispered.

She accepted that and lifted her lips to him. She remembered the girl who had been his first love but Pat was a generous woman, once she gave of herself. She'd never mention his earlier love and if he mentioned her she'd simply listen. She knew no vital living, loving woman ever had to fear a dead one.

'And I love you,' she told him quietly, when they moved apart. 'I think I have loved you for quite a time, Will. It's possible for a woman to love and fear at the same time.'

'Is there still some fear?'

She smiled at him. 'No. Not any more.' She turned, pulling him along. When they stepped inside the little old lighted room she released him and smiled when John Weldon's wrinkled face broke into a broad, happy grin.

CHAPTER TWENTY-ONE

The following day he drove over to take her into the nearby town. He had to buy their wedding-ring. He also confided that he had to buy a new suit. His wardrobe was limited to functional clothing; he'd had no thought at all of marrying when he'd bought it several years previously, after leaving the sea.

Her father wanted them to bring him back a special tin of tobacco, which they of course agreed to do, and sped away.

It was another of those bright winter days. Will glanced suspiciously upwards a time or two saying he had his doubts about all this lasting, and sure enough, along towards mid-day when they were in the town, clouds began to steal silently in from the west, great fat, billowy clouds with a hint of sootiness on their undersides.

But the warmth remained, the sun did not hide, and by the time they'd made their purchases and were ready to go back, although it was mid-afternoon and the clouds were still up there, scarcely moving at all, the sunshine never faltered.

He didn't mention something which had been uppermost in his mind all day until they were speeding homeward over a fine new carriageway. Then he said, 'I spoke to the registrar this morning.'

She waited, sitting close beside him. He looked round, saw her expression and plunged on.

'He can perform the ceremony almost any day of—next week. I've got a special licence.'

He'd stumbled a bit over the last two words. She slipped her arm under his and put her head upon his shoulder. 'What day would you prefer?' she murmured.

He was quick to protest her docility. 'It's not for me to say, Pat. It's for *you* to say.'

She was silent and relaxed with a little slipstream of wind ruffling her hair through an open window. She gravely considered the roadway on ahead without really seeing it.

'Tomorrow week, Will?'

'Tomorrow week,' he murmured in confirmation, and both hands upon the steering-wheel tightened. 'That won't give a whole lot of time though, for bridesmaids, the reception afterwards, things like that.'

She smiled, sighed and moved her head slightly against his shoulder. 'My father will have the reception at our house. As for the bridesmaids and all that, I don't really care. I never wanted a large wedding.'

He seemed relieved. He said, 'Your father will give you away of course?'

'He'll be delighted, Will.'

They cruised under that lowering sky all the way back to Harlham where he finally had to switch on his head-lamps as they left the main road and took a plunging little downward ramp that shunted them out upon a more ancient, less manicured, crooked and familiar roadway. Harlham was lighted before they reached it, dusk was coming in fast and there was an increasing chill in the air, something they

234

both noticed as he drove round to her house and stopped.

As he alighted to run around and open the kerb-side door for her he glanced upwards. The clouds were moving, finally, sailing through a sea of invisible high wind like great galleons.

'Rain,' he pronounced.

She glanced up, less concerned. She couldn't have cared if there'd been another deluge on the way. He caught her like that, head tipped, heavy lips softly closed, brown eyes softly glowing with a sheen of total contentment, total acceptance. She responded to the touch of his mouth with a quick little savage fire, meeting his gentleness with her passion and her want. It threw him off; he put both arms around her drawing her so close the breath shattered against his face as he squeezed.

Then it was past, they stepped back and, shaken, looked at one another. She didn't drop her eyes from the look on his face. Gradually the fire left, he let out a little ragged sigh and said, 'What was I saying before that happened?'

'Something about rain.'

'Yes; well, let it rain. I couldn't care less.'

They laughed. He took her to the door and left. She went inside where her father peered over his glasses from the parlour. She strolled on in where he expectantly sat waiting.

'Did you find a nice ring?' he asked.

She sank into a chair nodding. 'And a new suit, and a few other things.' She kept looking at her father. 'How could I ever have been so wrong for so long a time?'

He put the book aside, removed the glasses as he folded them, he said, 'Well, I've never known anyone who learned how to loathe something who didn't also suffer as a result from biased judgement. When we go to war we don't hate an enemy government—we hate everyone living under the government. I'll admit its emotionally irrational to be like that, but I'm afraid it's quite human as well.' He waited a moment but when she sat without speaking, he also said, 'I've an idea that with beautiful girls it becomes rather easy to loathe young men. They see you at once as being desirable. They let you know how they feel in dozens of ways. The danger is to lump them all in the same unflattering category. As you know, Pat, all men *aren't* identical. What worried me was that you'd eventually become one of those vinegary spinsters who wouldn't and couldn't change.'

'Do you approve of Will?'

'Without any reservations.'

She put her head slightly to one side. '*Any* reservations, father?'

'Well, of course no father ever fully approves of the man who will take his daughter away from him. I suppose it works the other way around as well; no mother likes to see her son beguiled by some scheming girl. But for my own part, I'm perfectly satisfied. He'll make you an excellent husband. He'll be a good father, a sound provider, someone to lean on. He's strong and sensible.'

'And brave.'

'Yes.'

'And handsome.'

Old Brewster tucked away his spectacle-case, cleared his throat and let that one go by.

'And—so gentle.' She jumped up. 'How is Catherine?'

'Fine. She's been up and about a good deal of the day. In fact I believe she's in the kitchen just now.'

She was. When Pat walked through from the pantry she looked up quickly, half expecting to be scolded if one could judge by her expression. But Pat didn't scold. In fact she favoured early exercise for someone in Catherine's circumstances.

'I was getting supper for your father,' said the girl, and glanced at a wicker clothes-basket as she spoke.

Pat went over and looked into the basket. The baby was soundly sleeping in there on top of a carefully folded heavy towel. He had another towel over him. Pat was pleased with the improvisation and said so, smiling.

Catherine's apprehension vanished. 'Your father told me about your plans, Miss Brewster. I think it's simply wonderful. Absolutely spectacular. Mr Forman is so—manly. So handsome and strong.'

Pat went over to the kitchen table to help prepare supper. She and Catherine got into an easy conversation. The younger girl said she'd be going back to her room the following morning and when her husband came home she'd see that he came straight around and settled with the Brewster's for keeping Catherine and the baby all this time.

Pat said there'd be no charge; that whether her father ever received a penny through National Health or not for the use of his home as a lying-in place during the freak storm, didn't matter in the slightest. She was doubtful whether he'd accept payment anyway. He was, she said, a very independent man.

'One of the older generation, Catherine, who believe in standing unaided upon one's own feet.'

They kept coming back to the topic of marriage and at least on this topic the younger girl was far more experienced. She gave Pat all her secrets about making it a success. She and her husband had been married almost eighteen months earlier, which wasn't actually a very long while, but to Pat who'd never been married at all, it seemed a respectable period.

Pat's father came out after a while and joined them. He said he was hungry and the aromas were diverting him from his book.

It was a pleasant hour for all of them, then Pat heard the first fat drops and went to a kitchen window to look out. As she turned, it came to her that the mention of rain would dampen the spirits of her father and little Catherine Everett. There was something ominous now, about that most mundane of all words.

Her father, reading her face, said, 'Well, it's no secret really, Pat. I've been watching the clouds building up all the afternoon.'

He didn't sound the least bit upset. Catherine didn't either when Pat returned to the table. She said, 'Your father took me out in the garden to point out the different kinds of clouds. Cumulus...' she smiled weakly at old Brewster. 'I don't remember the others. Anyway, he said this can only be a brief shower.'

Pat looked at both of them. *They* were perfectly calm and *she* wasn't. It was humorous.

The ate on and although the rain began to fall steadily they only heard it when a little gusty breeze slapped it against a kitchen window.

It had a different sound too, slower, softer, as though these drops were fatter than the other ones. By the time they'd finished eating Pat's uneasiness was nearly gone.

It had vanished altogether about an hour later, when they were by the fireplace with the baby and the telephone rang. It was Will. He wanted to know if she'd had the radio turned on. She hadn't. She asked why he'd wanted to know. His reply came back in a droll tone of voice.

'To listen to the weather report. The entire county is going to get a very beneficial rain lasting until perhaps midnight. The promise for tomorrow is clear and mild. Of course it had to be.'

'Of course,' she repeated. 'And suppose the weather report is wrong?'

'It'll still be a perfect day,' he said stoutly. 'A foot of water would be like wading in ambrosia to me.'

She smiled at the blank wall. 'Couldn't you just settle for some *dry* ambrosia?'

But his call had calmed her last fear. She didn't even go searching about for the wireless.

Catherine and her father were discussing teething babies when she returned. There was a crackling fire in the grate. Pat kicked off her shoes, curled both feet under her in an easy chair and sat watching the leaping flames.

She heard every word her father and little Catherine were saying without retaining even one word in her mind. It must be wonderful, she thought, to have a loving husband who would telephone now and then for no more actual reason than Will had moments before.

She visualized him with a child in his lap. She pictured them walking through woods and across sandy beaches. She imagined them having a picnic in the autumn with leaves falling all round. She even thought of them working over the books in his shop and afterwards driving to one of the other villages to have supper.

The variety of things they would do together were endless. She was thinking of things which might happen years ahead, when her father, speaking her name for the second time, loudly, said, 'Pat, for heaven's sake stop day-dreaming and settle an argument for us.' She came back to the present with a slight start. 'Is it true that boy-babies get their first teeth earlier than girl-babies?'

She had no idea. She wasn't even certain any of her books would make that point clear. The safest way when pressed for an answer and in doubt which one to give, was always the diplomatic and non-committal one.

She said, 'It would depend upon the child. I'm sure William Paul will have teeth before any other child.' She smiled and they both laughed. Her father then went in search of his pipe and Catherine, using his brief absence to indulge in woman-talk, said, 'Miss Brewster, you were very wise to wait so long to get married. I should have only I just couldn't. Not that Harold isn't the one I'd have chosen three or four years hence, but with you and Mr Forman—well—it's just so natural. So perfect. You two were made exactly for each other.'

Pat said, 'Thank you, Catherine,' and fell silent for a sober moment reflecting on the fact that she hadn't really been waiting for the right man at all—or had she?

CHAPTER TWENTY-TWO

Will called at the house early in the morning on their wedding-day. He was wearing an open-throated white shirt, a light jacket and grey flannel trousers, all of it the casual attire of a man on holiday.

He wanted to take her for a drive in the country. She agreed although it struck her as a bit odd, this being their wedding day. But as though reading her thoughts he said, 'We'll be back in plenty of time. We haven't to be at the church until two this afternoon.'

The rain had stopped sometime in the late night or early morning. True to the prognosticator Will had heard, the sun was out, the clouds were nearly gone, the sky was soft blue and there was a delightful although slightly humid warmth in the January air.

They went directly through Harlham to the crossroads; one road was exclusively rural and meandering, the other arrow-straight and linking Harlham to the next village. Will turned off on the rural road.

She didn't care. It was quite early, they had most of the day ahead of them and as far as she was concerned their only obligations from now on and for as long as they prolonged a honeymoon, were to themselves.

He pointed out Esau Gibbon's farm. All the fields were well cultivated, sown with winter wheat and barley, except for one quite small field with sheep on it. There was a great mound of grim stone over there with trees, bushes and an untended hedge obscuring the entire thing.

Will saw her puzzled look and said, 'It's

a very old ruin. An ancient castle. No one knows much about it. I went out there the first year I was here. I didn't remember ever hearing of the ruin as a child.' He shrugged. 'If you happen to believe in the Arthurian legend, you can find local people who'll definitely convince you he owned that stone pile at one time. On the other hand if you prefer Harold or William, you can find supporters of the view that they erected the place. Not jointly you understand.'

He was laughing at her. She looked away as they moved on past, smiling. She liked his sense of humour. It was never boisterous nor overwhelming, but was always dry and pertinent.

'Which version do you prefer?' she asked.

He drove a short distance before answering. 'Frankly, I've wondered if in fact the entire thing wasn't erected by the Tourist Board which, having a great jumble of rocks left over from some restoration, dumped them here because Harlham actually has so little to be boastful of in the historic context.'

There was a low knoll up ahead with a superb view in all directions. He drove directly to it. There were three very ancient trees up there, wind-battered and warped, but sturdily alive. He stopped the engine, went round to hold the door for her to alight, then walked with her to the nearest huge tree and pointed outward where a torpid river, recently returned to within its ancient banks, was drowsily drifting along. There were villages far off, stone against greensward. She saw thin spires and in one place what appeared to be the ancient crumbling wall which had perhaps encircled a town.

'If I were a painter,' he told her quietly. 'I'd capture all this on a piece of canvas, take it home and hang it over my fireplace. But having no ability along those lines, I frequently drive up here to check and see that no one has changed it.'

'Has anyone changed it?'

'No. And if you'll sit here on my jacket I'll show you why.'

She sat, he dropped down upon the grass beside her, pointed in a general way and said, 'All the change which can be accomplished already has taken place. If you'll study the river you'll see it does upon occasion break out of its banks. No one would dare build any closer to it than they already have. A thousand years of living in that valley has taught people as much. And out where those rather larger villages stand—they doubtless were Saxon settlements, positioned in the most strategic places for defence and trade. All the land roundabout is for farming. No chalk in the soil; deep, well-drained.'

She smiled at his earnest profile, thinking he was so typically British it was no wonder he'd returned to his childhood village. He had that dogged pragmatism of his race, and although many Frenchmen, Germans, even Irishmen and Spaniards had categorically stated that there wasn't a drop of poetry in the British spirit, they were wrong.

It just wasn't an unearthly poetry that was all. Will loved this place, this view, this land, but he saw it as a blending of people and their environment, not as some unrealistic flight of poetic fancy. She could understand because she felt the same way, which she reflected was scarcely unusual since she came from the same stock.

Then he was finished and turned to find her studying him. He looked embarrassed, his smile was sheepish. 'Got carried away,' he muttered. 'Sorry.'

She leaned a little, kissed his cheek, straightened away and said, 'I've never been here before. I suppose I should say I hadn't the time nor the transport, but of course if I'd wanted to, I'd have come. I'm sorry now I didn't do it before.'

He covered one of her hands with his strong fingers. 'I'm glad you haven't. I know a dozen places like it where we can go. It's an interesting county. I even know of a lover's trysting place—or at least legend calls it that.'

She looked at him. 'Take me there sometime.'

He leaned back propping himself up with one elbow. The sunlight coming down through the wintry leafless branches above them made speckled shade and shadows. His strong, handsomely square face was gentle. He considered her minutely as though seeking flaws. There were none. The way she sat, knees drawn up, arms around them, dark curly hair close to her well-formed head, heavy lips softly closed, dark eyes liquid-soft in the winter sunlight, put him in mind of a Florentine cameo.

He said, 'I was wondering how much of all this we'll have together, Pat.'

She turned to gaze downward at him.

'Quite a bit I'd guess, although I've never taken your pulse to consider the condition of your veins.'

'Do you want to continue as local nurse?'

She shook her head slowly. She'd thought that out since her earlier discussion of it with her father. 'A married woman's first obligations are to her marriage.'

He agreed without saying so. She saw it in his eyes. 'And of course there'll be a family.'

She felt the colour climbing into her face, so looked out over the panoramic countryside again, saying nothing.

He reached, drew her down to him on the grass, put an arm under her head and bent forward. She met his lips with a tenderness that answered without a sound what he'd just proposed. Of course there would be a family.

For a moment they clung to one another, then he pulled back just a little and said, 'The world is full of dissatisfied people. Some call themselves transcendentalists. They aren't happy with what they are; they want to rise above the human estate.' He gave his head a little negative wag. 'I've seen 'em. Lots of 'em all over the world. They're small, insignificant, confused people. They're so eager to find something written in the heavens they can't see that for the brief space of a person's life the important thing is an old-fashioned, time-tested virtue. Love.'

She waited, knowing he had more to say. Up close his eyes were a darker blue than they seemed; perhaps, she dreamily reflected, that was because his hair was so black; some sort of inner reflection perhaps.

'Love of one's mate, one's offspring, one's environment. The creating of an environment for people—for you and me—that will last as long as we last. Do you agree?'

She agreed. He lay a hand lightly upon her soft throat. She closed her eyes at his touch. When he brushed his lips across her mouth she savoured his closeness with a thrill of longing. Afterwards, when he asked if she thought they should be going back, she rolled her head negatively upon his arm.

'Plenty of time.'

They lay side by side on the soft-scented earth gazing up through the leafless boughs where a cloudless sky hung in timeless array. She became drowsy and let her mind wander over what he'd said. She thought he was right; at least as far as *she* was concerned he was.

Others might rush pell-mell into the tangled vortex of emotional upheaval searching for the never-never land of ecstasy. She had once started on that path but hard sense had kept her going all the way. It had also made her face up to what she really wanted from life and it paralleled what Will obviously also wanted; a steady, unspectacular existence based upon the homely advantages: Home, husband, children, order, decency, the ancient virtues so much scoffed at in the present day.

She sighed softly. She had come a long way since innocent childhood, and she was fortunate that now, with her best years ahead, she'd found *the* man who would implement all her dreams.

He heard the sigh and felt for her hand to hold it. She squeezed. He squeezed back.

'You are confident?' he asked.

Instead of answering she raised up and leaned across him, found his mouth and clung to it. She was confident.

From somewhere a diaphanous cloud came drifting. It hadn't been there an hour before, but then neither of them had been watching the sky for that hour. When it floated across in front of the sun she opened her eyes feeling the difference. He looked upward also.

He said, 'It wouldn't dare.'

She raised her brows. 'Dare what, love?'

'Rain on our wedding day.'

She laughed, studied the floating transparent cloud and shook her head. 'It wouldn't dare.'

They sat up, saw that their view hadn't changed, got to their feet and stood a moment until the thin little cloud passed, letting sunlight come forth undiluted again, then they slowly made their way back to the car. It was noon. They had been four hours on top of their hill although it didn't seem half so long.

She told him it would take her an hour to prepare for the wedding, therefore she thought they'd better get back. He agreed, but when he slid under the steering wheel beside her he sat all loose and easy for a full minute gazing out where the sparkling world lay below.

'For some reason,' he told her, 'I don't

want any of these moments to end. I have a feeling that each one will be forever lost the moment we leave this spot.'

She understood and reached over to smooth the hair above his temple. She said nothing. Particularly, she didn't mention the time. After a bit, he turned, smiled, then started the engine and headed back. But he drove more slowly until they came within sight of that old ruin in a corner of one of Esau Gibbon's fields, then he picked up speed a little saying, 'The girl we left up there on the knoll and that man who was up there with her—will never meet again under that tree.'

'No. But a settled, stodgy pair of married people will meet up there again. Many times, I hope.'

He smiled a little and felt for her hand. 'Many times. I can promise that.'

Harlham was quiet in the noon-day sunshine. The Coach and Four was closed. At least the front door was closed which ordinarily signified John Weldon was not transacting any business in that section of his building.

There were a few people abroad and out in front of Frank Eaton's iron and scrap yard a small lorry sat with its load of rusted odds and ends.

She said that Harlham typified *her* Britain. He agreed, then, with a droll smile he suggested that perhaps both of them were out of step with modern Britain. 'I've never seen you wear a mini-skirt, although I'd love to.'

She had an answer for that. 'Don't you feel a bit cold, wearing your hair so short?'

They laughed at, and with, one another. Her father's house appeared dead ahead. Will eased to the kerb, switched off the engine and twisted a little. 'For the last time before we're married, I want to say how fond I am of you, Pat. How you've measured up in all ways to what I've always dreamed a perfect woman—and wife—would be.'

She leaned, closed her eyes and as his lips came seeking hers she said, 'I love you, Will.'

The publishers hope that this book has given you enjoyable reading. Large Print Books are especially designed to be as easy to see and hold as possible. If you wish a complete list of our books, please ask at your local library or write directly to: Dales Large Print Books, Long Preston, North Yorkshire, BD23 4ND, England.

This Large Print Book for the Partially sighted, who cannot read normal print, is published under the auspices of

THE ULVERSCROFT FOUNDATION

THE ULVERSCROFT FOUNDATION

. . . we hope that you have enjoyed this Large Print Book. Please think for a moment about those people who have worse eyesight problems than you . . . and are unable to even read or enjoy Large Print, without great difficulty.

You can help them by sending a donation, large or small to:

**The Ulverscroft Foundation,
1, The Green, Bradgate Road,
Anstey, Leicestershire, LE7 7FU,
England.**
or request a copy of our brochure for more details.

The Foundation will use all your help to assist those people who are handicapped by various sight problems and need special attention.

Thank you very much for your help.